# Also by Natasha D. Frazier

## Devotionals

The Life Your Spirit Craves

Not Without You

Not Without You Prayer Journal

The Life Your Spirit Craves for Mommies

Pursuit

## Fiction

Love, Lies & Consequences

Through Thick & Thin: Love, Lies & Consequences Book 2

Shattered Vows: Love, Lies & Consequences Book 3

Out of the Shadows: Love, Lies & Consequences Book 4

Kairos: The Perfect Time for Love

Fate (The Perfect Time for Love series)

With Every Breath (McCall Family Series Book 1)

## Non-Fiction

How Long Are You Going to Wait?

# Acknowledgements

My biggest thank you is to Jesus, who orders my steps, forgives my sins, and blesses me with the time and ability to do the thing I love – write.

And we've done it again! I'm excited about this series and my hope is that it shines through the pages.

To my mom – Thank you for your unwavering support. Each time I publish a book, I can still see you jumping up and down screaming, "That's my baby," just as you did when I won the trophy for highest overall average in third grade. I'm not embarrassed about that now. (smile)

My husband, Eddie, and my children Eden, Ethan, and Emilyn – thank you for sharing me with my characters.

Chandra – Thank you for your editing expertise. You are, indeed, the best.

My dearest reader – Thank you for reading, reviewing, and sharing my books with others. I am thankful for you and your support.

Natasha

# With Every Step

McCall Family Series Book 2

# <u>One</u>

In the twenty-first century, birth order still seemed to matter in the McCall family—well at least to the patriarch. No one else seemed to care, especially Darius McCall who viewed the idea as archaic—another tactic his father, Jeffrey McCall, used to straggle him along and keep him in his shadow as opposed to relinquishing the McCall Resorts chief executive officer title to Darius as he'd rightfully earned.

McCall Resorts started off as a family farm with one bed-and-breakfast and had evolved into a forty-two-hundred-acre luxury resort with sixty rooms and activities for guests that ranged from exercise and wellness to family craft events. And for the past twelve years, Darius had spearheaded the addition of most activities their guests enjoyed. Because of him, revenue had increased twenty-five percent.

That had to count for something—should have been a determining factor in deciding whether he or his older brother, Andrew, should run the business.

At five A.M., Darius ran along the one-mile path he'd designated as his get-his-mind-off-of-whatever-bothered-him trail. Sweat flew from his forehead in the sixty-degree temperature, but none of his tension eased. With every pound of his feet against the pavement, Darius' pulse got closer and closer to his maximum heart rate, but not because of the intensity of the exercise—he could run for at least an hour at six miles per hour. Every time he thought about his father simply handing over the reins of McCall Resorts to Andrew, Darius' fitness watch vibrated, alerting him to engage in breathing exercises.

Darius maintained his pace, coming upon mile three of his morning run. He shoved his wireless Bluetooth headphones deeper into his ears, leaning on the rhythm of the music to beat louder than his thoughts.

But it didn't.

He couldn't be sure if he was angrier with his dad or his brother, particularly since Andrew didn't want the job in the first place. He had his sights set on becoming a professor at Jackson State University. Now all of a sudden, Andrew and his wife, Nina, were happy at the family's resort and chose to stay and work in the family business.

*Give me a break.*

As he neared his home, the antebellum-style mini mansion, he slowed his pace, hunched over, rested his hands on his knees, and released calming breaths.

Andrew's façade would soon end, and Darius would get what he deserved.

He puffed out another breath. He hadn't worked as hard as he did for the last twelve years just to stand by and watch his brother reap the benefits.

∞

"Annette, alert me when my father and Drew arrive," Darius called out to his assistant on the way into his office without the courtesy of his customary "good morning" greeting. He'd been on edge since his father announced the deal to break ground on their second resort in Texas had reached the final stages. With financing secured, their next step would be meeting with the contractor.

Darius paced the expanse of his office whose size was comparable to that of a small studio apartment. Choosing the details of his office had been one of the perks of spearheading the buildout of the space. His father didn't object to any part of the design, giving Darius full control of the project, which had been another reason he didn't have any doubt that he'd be CEO, not Andrew's right-hand man.

He swiped the iPad screen, reading through the fine print of the contract with Slaughter Construction, Incorporated. Though alone, he mumbled his opinion about the contractor under his breath. For starters, why would his father hire some middle market construction company to do the job when a much larger company with more experience and resources could get the job done in less time?

Just another reason he'd be better as CEO.

Decisions like that were costing them money. The additional three months or so it would take SCI to complete the project could be three months where they were up and running with customers staying at the resort and the company reaping revenue from farming activities.

Three soft taps at the door halted his tracks.

"Come in."

Annette's silky elbow-length hair swung through the door opening before she did. "They're here. Went straight to the conference room and are waiting for you."

"Thanks, Annette."

"You're welcome."

"Oh, and apologies for my rudeness earlier. Good morning."

She smiled and waved him off. "Good morning, Mr. McCall. Would you like a coffee for your meeting?"

"No thanks. I'm alright for now."

Annette had worked with him for the past five years, so his mood swings weren't new to her, but that wasn't any reason for him to be rude. He'd change that since he didn't want to be the kind of boss his employees tiptoed around because they weren't sure what kind of mood he'd be in.

That was one prop he could give his father. No matter how he felt or what his personal issues were, he respected his employees and treated them kindly—remembered names, birthdays, children's names.

Annette ducked back out of the door and shut it behind her.

Like Mufasa showing Simba the expanse of his kingdom, chest puffed, chin lifted, and mind focused, Darius gazed out the window at the lush green acreage before him, the sheer beauty of it all intoxicating. One day, he'd be in charge of it all, just like he was meant to be.

Darius strolled out of his office and down the hall to the main conference room. Through the floor-to-ceiling window, he could see Andrew and his father sitting side-by-side chuckling. Since Andrew joined McCall Resorts' executive team, the two of them seemed to spend more time together, with his father acting like the proud papa whose prodigal son had just returned. When he entered the room, they settled. He frowned, his gaze darting between the two of them.

"What's going on? I could use a good laugh this morning." Darius unbuttoned his jacket and took the seat across from the two of them.

"Oh nothing, just sharing a funny story with Andrew about an incident that happened a while ago. Nothing to worry about. Now that you're here, we can get straight to business." Jeffrey clasped his hands and offered a silly smile, one that he'd given to Andrew quite a bit lately, which drove Darius mad, yet he pasted a lopsided smirk on his face and redirected his attention to his iPad.

"Okay, let's go. Where are we with SCI?" Darius asked.

"Who?" Andrew piped in.

Yet another reason Andrew wasn't fit to be CEO.

His attention was more focused on his wife, Nina, than his job as CEO, not that that was entirely bad, but he needed enough balance to run this company well. And if he didn't know a thing about the contractors, why was he even in this meeting?

"Your brother likes acronyms. That's how he refers to Slaughter Construction, Incorporated."

"That makes sense. Sorry I'm a little all over the place today." Andrew rattled his hands against the mahogany tabletop. "Nina and I have an announcement to share at dinner tonight, but I'm not gonna be able to focus if I don't get this off my chest." He glanced between the two of them to ensure he had their attention—always attention seeking in Darius' opinion. Since he didn't come home after college to work with the family, he received more than his share of attention whenever he visited.

Andrew chimed in, "I've reviewed the timeline for completion, and everything seems to be on target. I know you wanted this project completed sooner, Darius, but SCI's timeline makes sense and includes the necessary time for us to cover our bases. We don't have to rush this project."

*Like you rushed into marrying Nina? But you didn't hear me saying anything about that.* "Drew, I just want the project done right. I'm over the issue with the timing. What I am concerned about is this Miss Slaughter." Darius scrunched his eyebrows so hard that his head hurt while he scrolled through the iPad. Had he missed something? "I thought SCI was owned by a man."

Andrew looked at him as if he'd grown another head. "Does the owner's gender matter? You can't be seriously tripping out over that."

"Did I say that?"

"No, but the fact that you brought it up tells us it matters to you. That's pretty sexist of you."

Jeffrey piped in, "Darius, if you desire to be CEO—if Andrew changes his mind about the job—then you need to be able to work with anyone, regardless of the project and irrespective of their gender. This attitude goes against everything McCall Resorts stands for. If you can't handle this project because of Miss Slaughter, then tell me now. I won't allow you to lead my company if this is the man you've become."

"Hey, I can handle whatever comes my way. I think I've proven that over the last twelve years while pretty boy over here has spent the last twelve years proving just the opposite, yet I don't see you questioning whether or not he's ready to be CEO." Even at thirty-six years old, with the amount of experience he had, Darius was more than prepared to take his father's place. Andrew couldn't say the same.

"Look, bro, leave me out of your issues. I'm not jumping on this roller coaster with you today. You keep talking about how much you deserve to run this company, then act like it. You don't see me charging you up every chance I get."

Jeffrey's voice thundered throughout the room. "Enough."

He looked between his sons and shook his head, the corners of his lips turned down. "Darius, nothing has changed. As I've said before, Andrew has the right to step down from CEO, which he said he will consider after he's given the position a fair shot. If he determines it's not a good fit, but that he'd rather teach, then we'll discuss what that means for your future as CEO. However, that's not an automatic transition for you. You possess a wealth of knowledge, but this haughty attitude of yours, this sense of entitlement, and quick temper are not the ideal qualities for the face of this company."

Out of respect, Darius nodded and listened as his father spoke, but his gaze zoned in on Andrew. He clenched his jaw and took determined, even breaths. Jeffrey McCall hadn't been wrong about him showing qualities that weren't quite ideal for McCall Resorts' future CEO. Darius willed himself to stay in his seat when what he really wanted to do was hurl across the table at his brother and defend himself against his father.

Everything had been going his way until Andrew returned and messed things up. He'd been certain that he'd proven to his father that he could run the company, and before Andrew came trotting home, Darius had been convinced that it was only a matter of time before his father named him CEO.

"As previously discussed, the plan has not changed. This project will be one you'll run yourself. You'll be the face of McCall Resorts when it comes to any interaction with SCI. If you can grow from this experience and be the leader I know you can be, then we can talk more about you being CEO if Andrew decides to take his career here in a different direction. And of course, if Andrew decides he's exactly where he needs to be, we'll have to discuss other options for you."

Oh, with a new child on the way, Andrew had one foot out the door already. Despite the fact Andrew occupied the CEO position, Darius wasn't convinced that Andrew was interested in running the company. Andrew believed in purpose, passion, and all that jazz. Being CEO was far from it, so Darius' only obstacle was proving to his father once again that the job should be his—and should have been his from the beginning.

Regardless of what his opinions were about a woman-owned construction company, he wouldn't let them get in the way of him running his family's business.

# Two

Kennedy Slaughter commanded the attention of her employees, Vice President of Operations Chris Wilcox, and Superintendent Michael Stewart. Gathered around the cherry oak conference room table, she briefed her team on the McCall Resorts project — their largest project to date. Her deceased twin brother, Kendrick Slaughter, would have been proud of her for stepping into his shoes and closing such a massive deal. Her parents would also be proud, but they weren't alive to witness it either. She'd declared it her duty to make them all proud.

Her chest inflated at the thought.

But Kennedy didn't belong at the head of the table— not that one anyway.

She'd studied accounting and had been SCI's accountant for the last ten years, but Kendrick's death a year ago left her no choice but to step up. He couldn't be replaced, at least not in her eyes. She drew in a long breath to steady her nerves and addressed her team with a calmness she didn't feel. If anything went wrong with this project, it could potentially destroy their company with the bad publicity they'd receive. She couldn't imagine them bouncing back from it.

"Thanks for meeting me so early, Chris and Michael. This has been a tough year for all of us, and it's worth me saying that your hard work and commitment to SCI are much appreciated. As you know, the McCall team is in town to walk the property, so they're coming to our office for the first pre-construction meeting in about an hour. Are there any last-minute concerns we need to discuss before their arrival?"

Chris, a man twice her size with cold eyes—eyes that didn't convey his kind spirit—rested the weight of his forearms on the table and spoke first. "No issues about this project right now, but we do need to speak about the Blue Wing project later."

Kennedy massaged the back of her neck to ease the tension at the mere mention of the Blue Wing project, which had sucked money out of their business to the point they would barely break even. "Sure, Chris. I'll stop by after lunch."

Mike rapped on the table, and the light in his eyes reminded her of her twin brother. Mike's mother, Mabel Stewart, was her mother's best friend and SCI's receptionist. He spent so much time with her and Ken growing up that he was practically raised as their brother. They garnered strength from each other as they grieved the sudden loss of Kendrick. He was killed by the driver of an eighteen-wheeler who fell asleep at the wheel.

In fact, Mike had been stronger than her, and the continuing business operations could mostly be contributed to him. To get through his pain, he dug himself deeper into work—work at SCI was the one thing they agreed they could do to honor Kendrick's memory.

"I don't have much either than the fact I'm pumped to add a project like this under my belt. I've studied their Georgia resort online, and it's massive. My crews are lined up to get to work. I've already worked out the schedule, which I sent to you last week."

"Thanks, Mike. I looked it over and sent it to Mr. McCall to review. That'll be a topic of discussion for our meeting later." Kennedy offered a few closing comments and sentiments of gratitude before concluding their meeting. "If there's nothing else, I'll see you two back here in forty minutes to meet the execs of McCall Resorts."

Chris didn't waste any time pushing away from the table and retreating to the break room for his second round of coffee. Mike lagged.

"So how are you really? And don't give me semantics. This is the first big job since we lost Ken. How're you feeling about it?"

Kennedy sighed and folded her hands into her lap, secretly rubbing the perspiration on her pant leg. She hid her out-of-control pulse and clenching stomach behind what she hoped to be a reassuring smile.

Of course, she was a ball of nerves.

At thirty-seven years old, her life didn't quite look like what she'd imagined for herself ten years ago, or even five years ago. She'd been thrust into the position of SCI's president to fill her brother's shoes—shoes that were too big for her dainty, unqualified feet.

"I'm feeling pretty confident."

Not entirely true, but as the boss, she held on to the adage *fake it 'til you make it*. "Like you, I've been studying their resort in Georgia and combing through this contract. You know I'm not Ken, so I have to really study this stuff, but I can handle it. Besides, I can count on you to help me if needed, right?"

"I got you." Mike tagged her shoulder. "And if anyone hasn't told you, you're doing a good job. We have a pretty solid team who was loyal to your brother and will be loyal to you."

"Thanks, Mike."

"No problem. I know this isn't the role you were trained for, but you've got this, and you've got me out there in the trenches handling thangs." Mike stood and squeezed her shoulder. "Just let me know if you ever need anything, okay?"

"Will do." Kennedy covered Mike's hand with her own. "Thanks for stepping up around here. Now go get your coffee and get settled before the big meeting."

Mike left the room and shut the door behind him. Though grateful to have him by her side, Kennedy almost couldn't deal with how much Mike reminded her of Ken—

their stature, warm cocoa eyes, and comforting voice. And most of all, their faith in her abilities. Hopefully, the McCall family would find her capable as well.

∞

Kennedy replaced the phone on the receiver after Mabel Stewart, SCI's office receptionist, called to make her aware that the McCall Resorts team had arrived. She smoothed her hands along the buttons of her suit jacket and squared her shoulders.

Poised.

Precise.

Prepared.

She strutted into the office lobby and thanked Mabel who sat behind the receptionist desk. Three pairs of strikingly similar eyes locked on her. Her pulse sprang into a sporadic rhythm like a racer who'd just lurched into a full-on sprint. *You've got this. The only one questioning your abilities is you.*

"Good morning. You must be Kennedy Slaughter. I'm Jeffrey McCall, owner of McCall Resorts. These are my sons, Andrew McCall, CEO, and Darius McCall, COO and project manager."

"I'm Kennedy. Pleasure to meet you all." Kennedy framed her face with her brightest smile and shook each hand in the order introduced. Thank goodness for the practice of giving a firm, confident handshake in business school because they took no mercy when squeezing her hand. When she shook the last McCall's hand, an indescribable warmth snaked up her arm.

Almost familiar.

Almost like their hands were made to be held by each other.

Something told her the feeling was mutual because for a millisecond, he paused the shake and hiked one eyebrow, like she could give him answers about what had just transpired between them. The right corner of his lip tilted upward, and something she couldn't identify slithered through her.

She swallowed to cure the dryness in her throat.

Kennedy slid her hands out of his grasp and resisted the urge to run her hand along her pant leg.

*You're in charge here. Don't forget that.* "Would either of you like coffee or water before heading to the conference room?"

Jeffrey and Andrew requested water.

Darius, the one who lit her hand, head, and heart on fire in a matter of seconds said, "I'll take coffee, if you don't mind."

Mabel rounded her desk and moved to where the group stood. "I'll go grab that coffee for you. Cream and sugar?"

"I don't mind making it myself. I'm a little picky." Darius chuckled and sent ripples to Kennedy's toes.

"Please follow me to the break room so we can get you that coffee. I'll escort him back to the conference room."

Mabel to the rescue. Though Mabel always took care of their customers' refreshment needs, Kennedy couldn't have been more thankful for her in that moment. She could foresee an extra minute alone with him becoming awkward, especially after that handshake, with her reverting to that awkward, clumsy, college-aged girl tripping over her words and feet, probably running the man and his family out of her office.

"Thanks, Mabel."

Inside the conference room, Kennedy engaged in small talk with Jeffrey and Andrew. Weather and travel to Houston. After a couple of minutes, the tension in her shoulders eased, and she relaxed in her seat. Maybe everything really would be fine and she'd been on edge for no reason at all. She could appreciate the fact that her gender didn't seem to be an issue. She'd had that issue with the Blue Wing project and several others who preferred to talk with anyone on SCI's team but her. She didn't get that impression from the McCall team, which meant they were off to a good start.

Mike and Chris filed into the room and took seats to her right while Darius followed and sat next to his father, Jeffrey. Kennedy introduced her team to the McCall family and trudged forward according to the meeting agenda.

Kennedy hit the side key of her tablet to illuminate the screen.

"First, just let me say again that we are pleased you've chosen SCI for your construction needs. We're committed to managing all phases of your project from here through post-construction use of facilities. If there is anything we can do throughout this process to make things smoother for you, please let us know. Now…"

She paused to take a breath and calm herself after realizing her words were rushing out of her mouth like water from a faucet on full force.

"If you'll turn to page two of the binders before you, let's go through each phase of the project. Of course, this is phase one and the planning and design are complete. The next steps will be for SCI to get permits from the city for your build. We already have contractors in place who are ready to start. Mike, our superintendent, can tell you more about that."

Kennedy opened the floor for Mike to discuss the permitting process and answer any questions the McCall team might have. She'd only sat in on one of these meetings when her brother started a new project, which helped her to some degree, but Mike was the more knowledgeable person, and that became more apparent the more he discussed the pre-construction process and permitting. He held everyone's attention, except for Darius who seemed to be focused on her. If his eyes held the power to sear a hole into her head, she'd be dead by now.

She shifted her attention to Mike, hoping that Darius would do the same, but he didn't. Instead, his laser beams engaged her as his target. He didn't smile, so she couldn't read him. Was he staring because he didn't trust in her abilities, or was there a mutual attraction?

If attraction wasn't the entire reason he focused on her, even when he should have been paying attention to Mike, it was part of it.

No matter the case, this project was the most important thing to her right now; everything else was irrelevant.

"As we enter the construction phase, delays can happen, and though we can prepare for them, we can't control things like inclement weather. If there are weather conditions that will affect our timeline, that'll be communicated to you. Though we want to complete your project timely, we also want to do it right, managing materials, resources, and operating within your budget constraints."

There went the frown on Darius' face. The word *delay* must have been his hot button because his bottom lip curled, and his crinkled eyebrows froze in place.

"Thanks, Mike." Kennedy powered through the agenda, discussing how the project would be managed and opening the floor to Chris to discuss his role of overseeing operations, staffing, and project management. She relaxed in her seat, a proud smile spread across her features. Their audience, Jeffrey and Andrew McCall, seemed pleased with what they'd heard. Nods and reassuring smiles. Darius, on the other hand, didn't seem convinced.

*What's his problem?*

As much as Kennedy didn't like to put herself in a position to answer a question she didn't have the answer for, she sought to ease Darius' worries, whatever they were.

"Darius, do you have any questions? You seem a bit concerned."

He pounced forward against the table, steepled his fingers, and pointed them in her direction. "There is one thing you can answer for me. I'm curious. I've read your bio on your company's website. You seem to be new to your position. I also noticed that your testimonials are from businesses with projects a lot smaller than this one. How can you assure us that it will be done to our satisfaction?"

Mike poised himself to interject, but Kennedy raised her hand to defend herself.

*So that's what the staring was about.*

"Mr. McCall, this is my first year as president of SCI, but I can assure you I've worked in this business for the past ten years, so I'm not new to this. Combined, Mike and Chris have more than twenty years of experience and come highly recommended. Would it put your heart at ease to personally speak with some of our past clients?"

"No, Miss Slaughter, that won't be necessary," Jeffrey intervened. "We've done our due diligence and are more than confident that SCI can handle this job. Please don't take any offense to Darius' comments."

Kennedy pasted a smile. *He's not the first man to question whether I belong here.*

"None taken. My work has and will speak for itself." A quick glance toward Mike, and he nodded his approval. She stood her ground, something she knew she'd have to do at some point in this project, probably because she questioned herself, but Darius didn't know her and didn't have the right to do so.

"I'm sure that it will." Jeffrey closed his binder. "We don't have any more questions at this time."

Mike stood, strode around to the other side of the table, and extended his hand. "Thanks for your time and your business. We'll be in touch when we receive the permits to confirm groundbreaking."

"Yes. Thank you. May I buy you lunch before your property tour?" Kennedy offered because it was something her brother always did after meeting with current and potential customers.

"Please," Jeffrey McCall said, patting his protruding belly, "lead the way."

Kennedy excused herself to gather her purse and keys and returned to find the group of men gathered outside the office in the elevator bank.

"Kennedy," Mabel called to her just as she reached for the door handle, "I'm proud of you holding your own.

Your parents and Ken would be too." There went that motherly I'm-so-proud-of-you smile and wink.

"Thanks, Mabel." Though they weren't blood relatives, Mabel had been a part of her life since she was born. She and Mike were the closest family she had.

Mike hit the elevator button when Kennedy joined the group. The smallest in stature, she felt like she could be their younger sister, but she had to remind herself she was the boss.

In control.

The leader.

Standing a foot behind her, Darius leaned closer to her ear while the rest of the group was engrossed in conversation about last night's basketball game.

"I have a lot riding on this project. I'm counting on you to get this done without any hiccups, so I hope you're as good as you claim to be."

The hairs on the back of her neck stood at attention. Her heart and stomach melded together at the sound of the low baritone voice close to her ear. She heard him loud and clear, but what he didn't understand was that she had a lot riding on this project as well. Whatever he had going on couldn't be more important than her honoring Ken's memory and setting this business up to take on even larger projects.

"Mr. McCall," Kennedy turned slightly and said, "I'm better than good."

"Prove it."

"You didn't even have to make the request."

The elevator arrived, and the group parted like dancers waiting to start a *Soul Train* line for Kennedy to enter first. Darius filed in next, never taking his eyes off hers as he entered. She didn't know what to make of him. Part of her perceived he was flirting, but she couldn't go there. Entertaining any romantic thoughts about him was a bad idea. Never mind the fact that he was handsome, and she'd likely see his heart-stopping eyes in her sleep. This project would not get ruined on any account.

Everything was on the line.

# <u>Three</u>

Darius didn't speak much on the plane ride back to Georgia. He mindlessly rubbed his beard and gazed through the window at the blue skies. His thoughts were consumed with Kennedy Slaughter. Kennedy had been feminine, beautiful, and nothing about her said she liked to get her hands dirty or even enjoyed the line of work she managed. He imagined she'd be the kind of woman interested in the arts—painting, writing, or even a professional dancer—but not construction work.

He couldn't help the comments that slipped out during lunch and then during the tour of their property. Honestly, he'd dismissed her as being qualified, which she later displayed, the moment he laid eyes on her in the lobby of SCI and furthermore at the jolt of electricity that coursed through him when they shook hands.

There was no denying she felt it too.

If she didn't, she had him fooled by the way her gaze lingered a bit longer after addressing his questions during their meeting. Or the delicate squeeze of his hand during their goodbye-nice-to-meet-you handshake. Her grip was softer than it had been upon their initial greeting. Not a business handshake, but the kind where she practically rested her hand in his like she wanted him to press his lips against the softness of it.

But perhaps it was his vivid imagination interfering with reality. Kissing the back of her hand was all he wanted to do and would have done if their circumstances had been different.

"Darius, how're you feeling about the project? I know SCI wasn't your first choice, but are you more comfortable now that you've personally met their team?"

Andrew snapped Darius out of his thoughts of Kennedy. His dad cut him out of the final decision-making process when hiring SCI—yet another move that was unfair to him. He'd been by his father's side far too long for his voice not to count.

"Yeah. I liked Mike and Chris. Their bios on the company's website are impressive, too. How many more trips do you think you'll make out here?"

"I'm not quite sure yet. Besides, this is all you. I want to be around for Nina in case she needs me. The last few weeks of this pregnancy have been rough on her."

Just like Darius thought. Andrew would stick around for Nina—as he should—which would start to give way for his opening to become CEO.

"I understand. Family first. You gotta do what you gotta do. Besides, this is my project, so I'll be staying in Houston for a while once we break ground. That should give you time to run things in Atlanta without me interfering or breathing down your back. Think you can handle that?"

Andrew chuckled and repositioned himself in his roomy first-class seat. "You've taught me well."

"Did you have any doubt that I would?"

"Nah. You know this business like you know your reflection. No one would question that." Andrew turned to him again as if he'd just had a lightbulb moment.

"So wait, you liked Mike and Chris, but what about the boss? Seemed pretty impressive to me—like the kind of woman who won't stand for you putting her in this box you have for women."

"I don't know what you're talkin' 'bout."

"Yeah, you do. You practically charged her up, challenged her on everything she said during lunch and the land tour."

"I would've done that to anybody in charge of this project. Man, woman, young, old, black, white, purple."

He would have, too, but not to the extent he'd done to Kennedy, to the near point of insultation.

"I doubt it, but just so you know, I wouldn't have jumped in if she slapped you a time or two. She's definitely a professional, I give her that, because you were borderline rude. I hope you have your act together the next time you come out here. Not sure you two won't be fighting before project completion."

"Man, whatever. Ms. Slaughter ought to know the rules of the business. If she wants to play with big boys, she's gotta have big boy knowledge. I applaud her though. She does know her stuff."

"Is that your side handed way of saying you were impressed by her?"

Darius snorted. "I think I'll reserve my compliments for now. Let's see how she handles the project from here on out."

Jeffrey, who Darius thought was napping, rose and joined the conversation. "Oh, she'll handle it well just so she can prove you wrong. She'll make you eat every rotten thought you had. She's kind, but her reputation precedes her. What does it say about a woman who doesn't miss a beat and steps in and runs her brother's company after he died?"

Darius shrugged one shoulder.

*The kind of woman who is about her business.*

"I suppose that's honorable. She's a quick study—jumping from the accounting department to president of SCI. But look here, as long as she holds her men accountable and they get this job done right and on time, I have no beef with her."

Jeffrey stepped forward and gripped Darius' shoulder. "Keep your eyes on the prize, son. That's all that matters. I'd hate to see you become distracted over something as miniscule as who the president of SCI is, especially when it has no bearing on project completion."

Andrew smirked and shifted in his seat to rest as if his job was done, which gave Darius the feeling that something else was going on he didn't know about. He gave Andrew's side profile a once-over. Maybe he needed to keep an eye on him, too. After all, he'd been full of surprises lately: elopement, child, willingly accepting the CEO position.

With Jeffrey back in his seat and Andrew minding his own business, Darius whipped out his iPad, tapped and swiped across the screen until he opened a search page littered with results for Kennedy Slaughter. Convinced it was just as important for him to know as much about her as he did about the Texas resort project, he tapped links and combed through articles about her and her brother's achievements.

He smirked when he came across an article that confirmed his initial assessment of her. She did have a love for dancing and danced for local theatre through college until she sustained an injury that prevented her from dancing again. He found himself smiling back at the photo of her, which was bright enough that it practically jumped off the screen at him. Could he get her to one day smile at him like that?

Darius hit the side button to dim the screen and shoved the tablet away into his briefcase.

This was strictly business.

His only goal had been to learn more about her from a professional standpoint, nothing personal, but his caged heart betrayed him at the sight of her—from the moment they shook hands to a moment ago on an electronic screen.

Kennedy Slaughter was off limits for romantic pursuits.

Completely off limits.

All he needed from Kennedy was to ensure this project ran smoothly and not cause him any trouble that would have his father question whether he could play nice and keep a level head. No matter what, everything depended on how things went with Kennedy and SCI, so he wouldn't mess it up. His piqued curiosity didn't scream louder than his long-term goal of becoming CEO.

Nothing could get in his way when he was so close he could smell it, taste it, and feel it.

Not even the beauty and graced wrapped up in Kennedy Slaughter.

# Four

"No, no, no." Kennedy groaned, slammed the telephone receiver back in its place, and buried her head in her hands.

What would Ken do in a situation like this?

How could this project go from being two weeks ahead of schedule to potentially two weeks behind? Mike's crew on the Doberman office building project were all down with the flu except for one guy. One person couldn't complete the job. And just how would this unfortunate circumstance affect their start of the McCall project? The last thing she needed was Darius McCall breathing down her neck and blaming this on her in some way. From their last conversation, he'd made it known he believed she was unfit to handle the job.

Kennedy practiced her meditational breathing for several minutes, then called Mike again, this time with cleared head space.

"Okay, speak to me like you're speaking to a kindergartener. What do we have to do to get this project finished, and how can we ensure it doesn't interfere with the McCall project?"

"I know you're the boss and this seems a bit out of control, but these types of situations happen all the time. It's one of those uncontrollable events we discussed with the McCall team. But for your peace of mind, we'll still finish the Doberman project on time. If you like, I can swing by to pick you up so that you can take a look for yourself."

"I trust you, Mike."

"I know you do, but operating on this side of the field is still new to you, so I'm picking you up in thirty minutes."

Kennedy released a steady, thankful breath. She didn't want to become the overbearing, micromanaging boss, but all eyes were on her to see how she would lead the company now that Ken was gone. And she couldn't afford any surprises, especially ones she didn't know how to fix.

"Okay, that's fine. I'll be ready. Just buzz me when you're here."

"Got it."

"Oh, and Mike, what about the McCall project?"

"We're waiting on one last permit, which I expect this week, then we'll be ready to break ground. I'd planned on sharing that with you when I picked you up. Figured you could use some good news since you're on edge about the Doberman gig. And to further ease your worries, the Doberman project won't have any effect on the McCall Resorts project because the contractors we hire to break ground aren't the same contractors we use to paint, which is where we are now on Doberman."

"You know I just need everything to work out with me being the new boss now and all."

"I told you, you're doing fine, but remember that me and Chris, along with everyone else know what we have to do. We got this, and we got you. We ain't gon' make you look bad."

Kennedy chuckled. Mike had been using that same line since Kendrick formed SCI, and thankfully, he'd been true to his word. Mike received more compliments than any other person on their leadership team. She liked to think of him as the glue that held everything together—the glue that kept the business going in Kendrick's permanent absence.

"Thanks, Mike. I know you won't. Thanks for that news. Honestly, that makes me feel better and will provide some comfort to Mr. McCall. I have a call with him later this afternoon."

"Sounds good. I'll catch up with you when I get there. Traffic is crazy, so I need to focus on the road."

"You do that. See you shortly."

∞

Kennedy strolled through SCI's entrance, mentally preparing for her next meeting. She'd just met with Mike and now she was prepared to update the McCall team.

"Darius McCall rang you about fifteen minutes ago. I patched him through to your voicemail."

Why was he calling her an hour before their scheduled meeting? Kennedy masked her displeasure with a tight smile. "Thanks, Mabel."

"Wait. What was that about?"

"Excuse me?"

"That li'l look you gave just now. Fluttering lashes and rolling eyes."

Oh, so she couldn't hide her displeasure.

"Nothing. I'm good."

Mabel stood and rounded the oversized cherry wood desk and came face-to-face with Kennedy, halting her tracks. "I've known you all of your thirty-seven years on this earth. Why are you so flustered by Mr. McCall?"

For a split second, Kennedy thought to feign innocence and ask which one, but only one of the McCall men got under her skin and made her heart thump like the speed of a jackhammer. She hated when Mabel sized her up like that—arms folded across her chest, head cocked to the side, and eyes zeroed in on hers like she could read every thought. Just as Mike had been like a brother to her, Mabel provided the comfort of a mother when she and her brother, Kendrick, lost their mother five years earlier.

"*Flustered* isn't exactly the word I'd use. More like *irritated,* I guess. He questions everything I do and say. We've hardly gotten this project off the ground. It's like he's waiting on me to mess this up."

"I can see a couple of things going on here, but we'll deal with the work issue for now. You doubt yourself, Kennedy. You were comfortable living in your brother's shadow here at SCI, but it's time for you to shine. Don't dim your light just because some man is uncomfortable with you being in charge because you're a woman. Show him your strength and how you know just as much about this business as him or anyone else."

"Thanks, Mabel."

"You're welcome, but I meant every word of it. You think we'd all be around here supporting you if we didn't think you could handle this job?" Mabel chuckled but Kennedy didn't doubt her sincerity as she pulled Kennedy into her arms for a tight squeeze. "Even if he does ruffle your feathers, don't let it show, because if you do, he'll keep at it just for the fun of it. I've met many Darius McCalls in my day."

Kennedy stepped out of her embrace, spun on her heels, and called over her shoulder, "The boss has a call to make. I'll talk with you later."

It was about time she acted like the boss and stopped clinging on to the shirttail of her brother who was no longer with her. She could run this business, and before this project ended, Darius McCall would be sorry he ever doubted her abilities.

Inside her office, she quietly shut the door behind her and settled into her leather executive chair before listening to Darius' voicemail.

*Ms. Slaughter, Darius McCall here. I know we're supposed to have a conversation in about an hour, but thought I'd call now since my schedule opened up. No worries though. I'll connect with you at our scheduled time. Thanks. Bye.*

If he hadn't been such a jerk when they first met, she'd swoon over the sound of his voice through the speaker. But being acquainted with the owner of that voice was like a splash of icy water to the face at the thought.

Kennedy clicked through her e-mails, reviewed Mike's notes, and replayed the conversation in her mind they had earlier today when she'd met with him. When it came to Darius McCall, she vowed to overcommunicate. Nothing could be left up to assumption or question.

One minute before their scheduled phone conference, she whispered a prayer and keyed in his number.

"Darius McCall."

"Hi, Mr. McCall. It's Kennedy Slaughter from SCI. How are you today?"

"I'm well. Thanks for asking. How are you?"

He must be in a good mood. She could feel his smile through the phone.

"Great. I met with Mike this morning, and I'm pleased to share that we're waiting for one last permit before we begin your project. Mike believes we'll get it later this week, but I don't want to make any promises. Just thought I'd give you a heads-up on where we stand."

"Well, that's good news. Are your contractors prepared to start immediately? I honestly don't want to waste any time."

"Absolutely. We're all good on our end, just waiting on the final okay from the city. Is it still your plan to be here for groundbreaking?"

"Yes. Nothing has changed. Now that we're getting closer, I'll make plans to move into my corporate housing next week."

*Move?*

Kennedy skimmed the project timeline document before her and discussed it with Darius once more. Yes, he planned to be in town for the next nine to twelve months while SCI constructed the resort homes, the Wellness House, restaurants, and leisure activity centers for resort guests. Kennedy could handle him from a distance—weekly phone calls to discuss the project—but the mere thought of him being physically present incited goosebumps along her arms and sweaty palms.

"Are there any other questions I can answer for you, Mr. McCall?"

"Not at this time, but do please call me Darius. We'll be seeing a lot of each other, and Mr. McCall is too formal for me. May I address you as Kennedy?"

"Yes, that's fine." Her voice lightened and held a hint of sweetness she didn't intend, which she quickly corrected. *Act like the boss.* "I'll be in touch."

"I look forward to it, Kennedy. Good-bye."

"Bye."

She replaced the phone and tapped her palm against her forehead a couple of times. In the span of thirty minutes, he'd almost made her forget the irritation he'd been to her and the fact that she was the boss and this was a business engagement. She had to be careful around the likes of him because she couldn't gauge his sincerity. Was he kind because he tried to make up for his earlier rude behavior, or did he have some trick up his sleeve to prove she couldn't get the job done?

*Bring it on, Mr. McCall.*

# Five

The last time Darius participated in one of the McCall family dinners, it ended before it even started. His mother, Rose McCall, threw together a celebratory dinner for his brother, Andrew, and his new bride, Nina, who had learned her illness wasn't fatal. He'd practically stolen their moment when he blew up over the fact that his father didn't value the work he'd put in over the last few years and still planned to hand the company over to Andrew.

Well, today would be different because this dinner was sort of a stepping-stone, a send-off in his honor.

The crackling of the fireplace and soft laughter greeted him at the dining room entrance. His parents were seated at opposite ends of the eight-seat rustic brown table with Nina and Andrew to the right of his mother and his place setting to the right of his father. A batch of his favorite honey butter croissants near his end of the table brought a smile to his face. His mother always knew how to reach him with food.

"For a moment, I thought I'd have to come up to your living quarters and bring you down myself."

"Sorry, Mom. Just took me a minute to get ready. Had to make sure I had everything in order." Darius strolled to her side and planted a kiss on her cheek, nodded his greeting toward Nina and Andrew, and squeezed his father's shoulder before rounding the table to take his own seat.

Rose sipped her glass of tea and rested her gaze on him. Darius knew that look, and so did his stomach because that sinking, hollow feeling in the pit of it followed, which he tried to suppress by scoffing down a croissant.

"My bad. You know these are my favorite," Darius said when his father cast a disapproving glance toward him because the food hadn't been blessed. Since he and Andrew were kids, the rule in the house was anytime someone took a bite of their food without praying first, that person had to be the one to bless the food. "Bless our food and our family. Amen."

"I hope we can expect you to have better manners and represent the McCall family well while you're in

Houston," his mother said, with an I-know-we-raised-you-better-than-that tone.

Andrew took a bite of his croissant and chimed in. "He could probably use a pep talk on how to respect women in power, but I have a feeling Miss Slaughter won't stand for any of his foolishness."

Darius shot him a warning glare, but Andrew continued. "He seems to think that the construction business is no place for a woman, especially Miss Slaughter. He practically charged her up on every detail of the project."

"Like I said before, I would have done the same thing if she were a man. Everyone at this table knows how important this project is to me. I'm not going to let her slide because she's a beautiful woman. She'll be treated just like any man would be. I expect her to be on top of her game."

"Beautiful?" Both Nina and Rose echoed and shared knowing looks before setting their sights on Darius.

"Ah, man. There y'all go. Don't go reading into this. Any man with eyes can see that the woman is attractive. I'm just saying that's not a reason to let her slide."

Andrew snorted. "And no one said that her looks were the reason behind your behavior, but now it looks like we're getting somewhere. It's not the fact that she's a woman, but a beautiful woman, as you put it. Dad, Darius might need supervision out there."

The McCall family erupted in laughter, including Darius. Though Andrew might have been joking, there could be some truth to his statement. As much as he'd been thinking about Kennedy over the past week, it was probably wise to have someone else around to keep him from mixing business with pleasure. All he could think about was exploring Houston with her as his guide and getting to know her as well as he knew the McCall business.

And he knew that business like he knew his reflection.

"Nah, Darius here is more focused than anyone I know. Not even Kennedy Slaughter can get him off track. That's something I'd expect from Andrew who's all about love and following dreams and passions. Darius is more like me."

"Is that right? I seem to recall a certain man sweeping me off my feet and begging me to run a farm and bed-and-breakfast alongside him," Rose touted and hiked an eyebrow. "If that's the case, there could be hope for Darius yet."

"Okay. I think that's enough about all of that. No more jokes at my expense. We're breaking ground next week. Can we just celebrate that we'll soon have two of the largest private resorts in the country?"

Darius lifted his glass of peach lemonade in a toast, which everyone followed. Largely due to the dedication and work he'd put in, his family's name and business had expanded far beyond the vision his father had when the resort first opened.

If he could strategize and strengthen McCall Resorts, surely, he could run the company as CEO and work alongside Kennedy without offending her or developing a romantic interest.

∞

Across the street from the McCall family's newly acquired strawberry, blackberry, and citrus farm, camera crews and reporters from local news stations were littered on the side of the road, covering McCall Resorts' milestone groundbreaking of their new family-owned luxury resort and farm.

Darius spotted Kennedy the moment he arrived, dressed more casual this time around in jeans, an SCI graphic shirt, and a straw hat. She waved him over. That woman could make a paper bag look good if she wore it. He plastered a half smile on his lips, waved to the spectators, but kept his gaze locked on Kennedy while he strode in her direction.

"Mr. McCall," she said, extending her hand, "all settled into your new place and ready to get this party started?"

He held her hand and crooked his head until she corrected herself.

"Sorry, Darius," she sang. "Ready?"

"Yeah. Seems I'm not the only one. This is quite the party." Darius folded his arms across his chest and nodded toward the television station vans. "Who invited the news stations?"

"We didn't, but I'm not surprised. This is a huge project that will create more jobs and bring a lot of tourists to the area. Besides, you seem like the kind of person who'd love this sort of thing—I mean the extra attention and all."

He chuckled a bit. After the heat he'd given her over the past month, he probably deserved a comment like that. And to be honest, he did enjoy that kind of attention. It was just the type of free advertising McCall Resorts needed to get folks excited about spending time in their new resort. Their marketing director planned a press announcement for when his father and brother would next be in town, but he'd be insane not to soak up every ounce of publicity the news stations would give him.

A reporter sporting a KHOU11 wind jacket interrupted their conversation, his cameraman on his tail. He introduced himself. Kennedy and Darius did likewise.

"Can we get a few shots of you two standing over here so we can get the construction vehicles in the background, and Mr. McCall, if you don't mind, we'd like to ask you a few questions."

Two hundred feet behind Darius and Kennedy, dozens of excavators began their dig. The cameras rolled, and Darius discussed McCall Resorts' vision of the luxury resort and even gave props to Kennedy and SCI who would help bring their ideas to life. In his peripheral, he caught the surprise on her face, but she recovered quickly and tacked on that professional smile she'd worn the moment they met.

When the reporters and camera crew were out of sight, Darius turned and snapped a few pictures with his phone and sent them to his parents and Andrew.

Darius and Kennedy walked alongside the dusty road and farther away from the noise of construction vehicles back to her car.

"Hey, thanks for the props back there."

"I wasn't wrong. You know your stuff, and I owe you that much. Just trying to make up for being rude to you when we first met—making up for a terrible first impression sort of thing."

"I appreciate that. Well, this is my car. You'll hear from me next week for our first of many weekly meetings. I expect this one to be short though. Mike and Chris will also be present to answer any questions."

"Thanks. Say, would you like to grab a bite to eat? My treat."

Kennedy whipped her phone from her back pocket to check the time and her calendar. The few seconds that passed seemed like minutes. Fifteen long minutes. It was crazy that he wanted to be a priority to her, like this project, but he couldn't expect her to drop everything for him. To ease the blow of potential rejection, he countered, "It's okay if you don't have time today. Maybe some other time."

"Actually, the timing is perfect. My next meeting is cancelled, so I'm yours for the next few hours. Is there any place in particular you'd like to go?" Kennedy opened the door, slid behind it, and used it as a buffer between them.

"A favorite of yours is just fine."

"You sure about that? I feel like eating a sandwich."

"Yep. You're my only friend in town, so I'm riding your coattail today."

Kennedy threw her head back and chuckled, a sweet sound he hadn't heard from her before, a melody to his ears. A carefree and casual tune that made him believe that maybe they could become friends.

"Zeroes it is. Follow me."

Darius hopped in his rental truck and trailed Kennedy to the sandwich shop. All the while, he couldn't stop thinking about how her laugh had done something to him. When they'd first met, she seemed so straight-laced and no-nonsense and poised for a fight whenever he brought up her qualifications or knowledge of the project.

But today, she was someone different.

From her clothes to her attitude. Laid-back. Friendly even. Maybe it was some reverse psychology to get him on his best behavior, but he'd already apologized for his mistakes. He vowed to himself and his family that he'd represent them well.

What it looked like he might need help with was keeping a reign on his curiosity about Kennedy. He hadn't been lying when he said she was his only friend in town, but the truth of the matter was somewhere deep inside, a part of him wanted more.

# Six

Kennedy welcomed the solitude the drive gave her from the construction site to the sandwich shop.

It gave her time to think, although about the one person she shouldn't be thinking about—at least not in the way her mind spiraled. Something about him had changed since he was last in Houston, even since their last phone conversation a week ago. He'd been kinder and less self-serving. Like the comments he made to the reporter.

*Kennedy here leads one of the fastest growing construction companies in Texas. Her knowledge and expertise is why McCall Resorts put their faith SCI's ability to lead the project in excellence. We're lucky to work with such a talented team.*

That statement had been nearly two hours ago, and her heart still fluttered. He may not have meant much by it and could have just been blowing smoke for the cameras, but boy, was he good at it. And then there was the lunch invitation, which wasn't uncommon with her clients, but none of her other clients looked like him.

Tall, dark, bearded, handsome with a heart-thumping, stomach-twisting smile.

She could get through this. If it weren't for this project, they'd probably be enemies anyway, given his old-fashioned view of women and their roles in the workplace. Though he'd toned his opinion down, she was sure if he had it his way, she'd be at home cooking meals, washing laundry, and taking care of every other household task.

Aside from his impeccable looks, he wasn't her type, so the next nine months should be easy as long as he kept his attitude in check.

Kennedy pulled into a parking space near the front of the restaurant entrance and shifted her car into park. Darius parked in the space next to her and was out of his car and opening her door before she could gather her purse and check her reflection.

"Thanks, but you didn't have to do that."

"I may have been a jerk and given you a bad first impression, but no matter what you think of me, know that I'm a gentleman. It's how I was raised. So yes, I had to open the door for you." He closed the door behind her, and Kennedy smirked but didn't take the bait. Her knee-jerk response was to ask if he'd been raised to talk trash to her, but as if he could read her mind, he continued, "And my behavior before was out of line, so again, I apologize for taking my frustrations out on you."

She sauntered ahead into the building, hopped in line, and looked over her shoulder, cutting her eyes at him.

"Apology accepted. Just don't let it happen again. There are other ways to channel your frustrations."

"I'd love to hear all about how you channel yours."

Kennedy shifted her attention to the cashier/order taker and requested a large smoked-turkey cheese sandwich, her favorite.

Darius leaned over her shoulder, close enough for her to feel his breath on her cheek, and handed his debit card to the cashier. She reasoned the only way he'd come so close was because he wanted to speak over the chatter in the restaurant. Not being one to read into things, she didn't miss the way he said it or how her stomach clenched at his nearness.

"Double whatever she's having."

"Thanks, but how do you know you'll even like what I'm having?"

"You seem like a woman who makes good choices. Besides, it's pretty hard to mess up a turkey sandwich."

"But do you like olives and mayo on your sandwiches?"

"As a matter of fact, I do."

Kennedy accepted their bottled waters and order number from the cashier and found a nearby table for them. Darius picked up the conversation they were having before they ordered their lunch.

"Your frustrations. How do you handle them?"

Kennedy shrugged and sipped her water. "Yoga, meditation, prayer, exercise."

Darius' eyes lit up. "You'd love the Wellness House that our resort offers. It's actually one of the most highly rated amenities we have. Guests are treated to massages, facials, plus areas for yoga, meditation, prayer, and exercise. You've gotta try it once we're up and running out here."

"Oh, don't worry. It's on my to-do list. I've researched the resort in Georgia, may even make a trip out there before this project is complete."

"So, what do you do out here for fun?"

A waitress attended their table with their sandwiches. Kennedy bowed her head and whispered a quick prayer.

"I hope you prayed for my food, too."

"Oh, I'm sorry. I didn't know whether that was something you did or not." She'd judged him again, but couldn't help it. Images of the jerk he'd been when they first met were hard to erase from her mind.

"Well, for future reference, I do pray—maybe not regularly, but at least before I eat—so keep that in mind for forthcoming breakfasts, lunches, and dinners."

Kennedy threw her head back and chuckled.

Darius joined her in laughter, but asked, "What's funny? I'm being sincere. You're literally the only person I know out here. You weren't planning to leave me hanging after lunch today, were you?"

Kennedy bit into her sandwich. *Yes.* That had been precisely her plan. The next time she shared a meal with him, someone else needed to be around—a third or fourth neutral party—to help keep her focused. Even though they sat in the middle of a crowded sandwich shop, it still felt too much like an awkward first date.

"We'll see each other for our weekly meetings, so I wouldn't necessarily call that leaving you hanging."

"Right. We'll be seeing each other every week for at least the next nine months. Tell me about Kennedy Slaughter. How exactly did you become president of a construction company? Has this always been a passion of yours?"

She was quite sure she briefly talked about it during their initial meeting, but he probably wasn't even listening. Kennedy bit into her sandwich again to shield the sadness that washed over her at thoughts of why she was sitting there instead of her brother, Ken. She chewed until the food slipped down past the knot in her throat and sipped her water. May as well tell the story one more time so that she hopefully wouldn't have to share it again.

"My brother, Kendrick, started SCI about ten years ago. This was his passion, his baby. I was his accountant, but he made sure I learned the business. He died in a car accident about a year ago, and he left SCI to me in his will. It's only right that I run it in his place. So here I am, doing my best to make him proud." Kennedy offered a weak now-you-know-so-please-don't-ask-me-again smile.

Darius reached over and covered her hand with his like it was the most natural thing for him to do, like they were actually long-term friends, or at least more acquainted than they were at the time. His eyes softened and that gorgeous, tender, lopsided smile teased the corner of his lip. This wasn't a date, but her heart and stomach didn't know the difference. The erratic pulses gave rise to the butterflies that seem to want out. She held her breath to steady her breathing. Maybe he wouldn't notice that his touch was doing weird things to her. Snatching her hand away would only put him on alert, so she left it there.

"I'm sorry about your brother, but for what it's worth, I think you're handling business well. He'd be proud of you, especially knowing that you didn't take any crap from me."

Kennedy giggled and fluttered her eyelids to keep the warm tears at bay. "Thanks. I appreciate that."

"You're welcome." Darius removed his hand like he suddenly remembered it didn't belong there, but his eyes held a hint of recognition. He'd felt his version of butterflies and constricted breaths. The quick rub of his chest had been a telltale sign.

Kennedy switched the conversation to lighter topics—topics that wouldn't lead to them touching in any sort of way. She couldn't take any more of that. His smile alone already had her thoughts teetering on the edge of confusing business with her personal life.

Maybe that was the problem.

She'd been so focused on running a business that she didn't make time to date. And now the first handsome guy who came along happened to be a business associate, and her heart couldn't tell the difference.

This business wasn't the only thing she needed to exert her authority over. It was time her heart learned who was in charge.

∞

The heat from Kennedy's hand seared an imprint in his. For the life of him, Darius couldn't reconcile what was happening between himself and Kennedy. He worked with beautiful women everyday back at home on the resort, but none of them affected him the way Kennedy had in the short amount of time he'd known her.

His heartstrings shredded as she shared about the passing of her brother. Though he had his issues with his brother, Andrew, he couldn't imagine him no longer being around for him to fight with. And he couldn't help but reach out to her. Had that table not been in between them, he would have pulled her into his arms and allowed her to cry on his shoulder.

Why was he becoming emotional around her and entertaining such thoughts?

Kennedy pulled her hand away like he'd scorched her and changed the subject. She'd been near tears. Did she pull away because of the connection she felt when their hands touched, same as before? But he chastised himself. What kind of man would make that moment about the two of them when it was obvious Kennedy was still working through her grief?

Kennedy interrupted his thoughts, reeling him back into the moment. "Tell me a little more about you. Have you been working at McCall resorts since you graduated college? Is running the family business all you've ever wanted to do?"

"Short answer, yes. McCall Resorts is all I've ever known. By the time I made it to junior high, I knew the business forward and backward. Not that it's hard, but I spent a lot of time by my father's side, sitting in meetings, watching him prepare reports and things like that. I've worked on the farm, planting crops and also reaping them. I bussed tables in one of our restaurants and worked in the kitchen in another. Managed some of the recreation activities like paintball and archery. Washed and fed horses. I even did a short stint at the Wellness House. I've fallen in love with that place and can't see myself anywhere else."

The smile that laced Kennedy's face made his heart swell. "I'm impressed. I never would have taken you to be the kind of person to get his hands dirty, but now I understand even more why this project means so much to you."

"Yes, it's a pretty big deal. Two years after graduating with my MBA, my father pretty much began to implement many of my ideas and became comfortable with my decision-making. So, it's been a total of twelve years. No one is more invested in this than I am—at least that's how I feel about it."

Which was also the problem he had with Andrew, a person who'd done the complete opposite but now occupied the position that was rightfully his.

"Well, SCI is with you up to and through the end. You're in good hands."

That, he didn't doubt. In fact, he knew he was in good hands when he held hers minutes ago.

Her cell phone rang, and she excused herself to answer it, but didn't leave the table. From her end of the conversation and the wrinkles in her forehead, something was wrong.

"Are you sure?…How are we gonna fix this?…How long will it take?…How could this happen?…I'll call you back in about ten minutes."

Darius didn't like the sound of that, especially when all he could think about was whether or not the problem she was having would impact his project in some way.

Kennedy tossed the phone back into her purse and massaged her temples. "Darius, I'm sorry we have to cut this short. I have a fire to put out."

"Is everything okay?"

"It will be. You've been good company. Thank you." She gathered her purse and water bottle and shifted her weight to stand. "I'll see you next week."

"Hey, I'll head out, too. Let me walk you back to your car." Darius tossed their trash in the bin, placed their red sandwich baskets in the designated area on a nearby table, and shuffled to keep pace with her.

Kennedy pressed the door unlock button on her key fob, and Darius reached around to open her door. She tossed her purse onto the passenger's seat and slid behind the wheel. War raged within him. His heart practically beat out of his chest, beckoning him to make plans with her before their meeting next week, yet his head ruled, reminding him that this was business and anything more would only be a distraction. Here she was having problems with something else, and his mind went straight back to his initial doubt of whether she could handle a job of this magnitude.

"Are you sure you're okay? Is there anything I can do to help?"

"Thanks for asking, but this is something I have to handle myself. I'll be in touch."

His feet were cemented in place until Kennedy backed out of the parking space and her car was no longer in sight. Darius climbed behind the steering wheel of his own vehicle with a solemn vow. No matter how attractive he found her, no matter the connection they seemed to share, nothing could come of it.

Nothing was more important than getting this resort up and running.

Nothing.

# <u>Seven</u>

One month down, eight to go.

Darius managed to keep his attention focused on the reason he was in Houston in the first place instead of diverting to Kennedy—though his heart wrestled with him every step of the way. Their weekly meetings were organized and succinct, which worked well for him because that left little time for his mind to wander off and give in to the what-ifs.

Today would be their fifth weekly meeting since the project began, and his father and Andrew were attending. His mother stayed home, but Nina traveled with the duo the night before. There was no doubt she would sit in on the meeting as well. Though Darius objected, Andrew couldn't seem to move without Nina by his side, giving the excuse that he wanted to be near her in case something went wrong. Given Nina's previous health scare, Andrew couldn't risk something happening to her and him not being around.

Yet, one more reason that Andrew wasn't prepared to be CEO. Though he sympathized with him, Darius believed Andrew needed to take a back seat instead of attempting to run McCall Resorts.

Jeffrey and Rose McCall didn't seem to mind Nina's presence in business meetings. They were of the idea that she was now part of the family, too. It couldn't hurt for her to learn as much about the business as possible.

Darius didn't agree.

But he was on a path to becoming a changed man, a more reasonable businessman, a leader who led by example, so he kept his snarky comments about her attendance to himself. In fact, he still wasn't convinced that she'd returned to Andrew's life out of her love for him, though trying to get his brother to see that was like teaching a cow to do dog tricks.

Darius dressed and navigated to The St. Regis to pick up the McCall crew for their morning meeting with the SCI team. As always, his father strode out of the revolving door entrance like he owned The St. Regis himself—tailored suit and shoes shinier than wet paint. And for someone who didn't want this life, Andrew fell into his role as CEO well with his pregnant wife, Nina, as arm candy sauntering alongside his father. Like they'd worked for this their entire lives.

Jeffrey and Andrew reached for the door handles, and Darius took a calming breath. What was it about their presence that brought him an insurmountable amount of anxiety?

*Be cool. This is a family business. Not your business.*

"Good morning, son."

"Good morning, pops." Darius offered a pleasant glad-you're-here smile, then tossed over his shoulder, "Morning, Drew and Nina."

Nina slid in first and squeezed his shoulder. "Morning, Darius. Good to see you."

Darius gritted his teeth and returned a forced smile.

What was wrong with him?

"Morning, bro. Let's get this show on the road. By the way, I appreciate how well you're keeping us in the loop and sending pics of the progress. Looking forward to seeing it with my own eyes today."

Darius turned his attention back to the front of the car and shifted it into gear. "Yeah, it's all good."

"The original resort is so beautiful and breathtaking, it's nice to be a part of the construction from the beginning. I can't wait to see the finished project," Nina added.

"I'm just honored my son here had the vision to help make this happen. You've been maintaining a good relationship with Kennedy Slaughter, haven't you? I don't want to walk in there blind today."

"No worries. Trust me. I've been on my very best behavior. I wouldn't dream of messing this up. Besides, she's actually nice to work with, and Mike runs a tight ship when it comes to managing the project and contractors. I'm pleased."

He glanced in the rearview mirror to get a look at Andrew, who eyed him back and hiked a doubtful eyebrow. Darius didn't verbally acknowledge it, but somehow knew it would come up later.

Thirty-five minutes later, after discussion about Nina's pregnancy—because yes, he had to at least show he cared about the well-being of his unborn niece or nephew and life back on the farm resort back in Georgia—they arrived at SCI's office building.

Inside, at the receptionist's desk, Mabel's eyes widened, and she sang, "Oh my word."

The McCall team looked from one to another and then back to Mabel, whose hands now covered her mouth.

"You're Nina Marie Robinson? The motivational speaker?"

Nina grinned and nodded. "Yes, ma'am, I am, although it's Nina McCall now." She pointed to Andrew, who stood next to her with the look of a proud husband.

"I've listened to you at least a hundred times, and I was in the audience when you spoke at the women's new year's brunch back in January. Thank you for telling your story. You indeed blessed so many of us. God bless you." She patted Andrew's arm, "And you, too, Mr. McCall."

Darius was seconds away from clearing his throat when Mabel seemingly remembered the rest of them and why they were standing inside SCI's offices in the first place. "Oh, I'm so sorry. I couldn't help myself. Didn't mean to hold you all up. Ms. Slaughter and her team are waiting for you in the conference room. Would either of you like water, coffee, or tea?"

The men declined, but Nina requested water. Mabel excused herself and whisked off to the break room. She returned with Nina's bottled water.

"Please follow me."

Mabel led them across the lobby and into the conference room where Kennedy, Mike, and Chris were seated. She stood at the door and whispered as Nina entered, "Can I please have your autograph?"

Nina nodded. "Sure can. I'll stop and see you on my way out."

Mabel peered around the McCall team filing into the conference room, waved to garner Kennedy's attention, and pointed to Nina. A fan-girl smile spread across Kennedy's face as well, but vanished, as if she remembered she was seconds away from conducting business.

Darius didn't miss Kennedy's lopsided, goofy, smile—a smile he hadn't seen on her before— and knew it had to be about Nina. She was accomplished in her own right, which he gave her props for, but those accomplishments didn't justify her seat at the table.

"Kennedy, Mike, and Chris, this is Nina McCall." He struggled to find the right words to describe her presence, yet hide his irritation.

Kennedy's smile faded as her eyes swooped down toward Darius' left hand, but she recovered quickly when Nina said, "This one. I'm married to Andrew." She jutted a thumb in Andrew's direction.

"Right." Kennedy plastered on a businesslike smile and nodded toward Darius. "We're ready to begin the meeting now. Does everyone have the agenda? We'll proceed as it's written unless anyone has any objections."

∞

Kennedy was proud of herself and her team. The meeting went well, and she hoped well enough that Darius forgot about the moment when her emotions betrayed her. She inwardly chastised herself for ogling the man's left ring finger in front of the entire team and allowing her disappointment to show when he introduced Nina as Nina McCall. There were three McCall men in the room. Obviously, it wasn't the elder McCall, but why did she automatically assume it was Darius?

Because she cared, that's why.

And she worked doubly hard these past few weeks to pretend she didn't. Not to mention, she'd read the news that Nina recently married. She would've remembered if it was Darius, yet her emotions temporarily took the wheel.

Hopefully, she didn't make a fool of herself the rest of the day. Next up was a tour of the project grounds, and then on for a business lunch. One thing sure to keep her mind off Darius was the fact she got to meet Nina. She often listened to her podcasts and YouTube speeches for encouragement after the passing of her twin, Kendrick.

Kennedy trailed Mike to the McCall project site, with the McCall team following her. She and Mike took separate cars because he would stay behind at the site long after the rest of them left. Thankfully, she traveled alone, which gave her enough time to encourage herself and repeat the reminders that Darius McCall was off limits.

Pulling into the designated area for contractor parking, Kennedy slipped her car into park and changed out of her pumps into a pair of gym shoes. She wore flats the last time she was out, and her feet still ached afterward. She stepped out of the car and joined Mike and the McCall team. Nina had the same idea, as she had changed her footwear into a pair of sneakers as well.

"Okay, Mike, I think we're all ready. Lead the way."

Mike led the group about a quarter of a mile down the road, huddled together like a six pack of soda cans so they could hear him over the sound of the construction vehicles.

"Here is the three-story office building. We estimate completion in another two months, as stated in the construction plan you have."

Directly across from the office building was ten acres of farmland, soon to be designated as the pick-your-own strawberries, blueberries, and citrus for resort guests. That was one difference between the Texas and Georgia resort, as their Georgia location did not have pick-your-own fruit activities.

At the end of the quarter-mile walk, Mike pointed out construction on either side of the road. "Here are the locations of both luxury estates, each of which will have nine bedrooms." He pointed ahead. "If you look down the road, you'll see pipes, and if you squint hard enough, the slab as well. We've laid the foundation for two private cottages. The work will start on those next week." He turned to face the group. "The next time you're out here, you'll need a golf cart or we'll have to ride in the car. It's coming along nicely."

"This is so exciting," Nina said. "I can think of many times where I could have used a place like this to come and relax, just to get away from it all."

"I'm with you on that. I can't wait to visit," Kennedy added. "Any questions for Mike? As of now, we're right on schedule, so that's good news. And like I mentioned in our meeting, we're still on track with the budget as well."

"I don't have anything, but if and when I do, I'll pass them along to Darius, and he'll share them with you," Jeffrey McCall boomed. A bright, pleased smile formed at the corners of his lips, and he slapped Darius' shoulder a couple of times.

"Andrew, any questions?"

"No, Kennedy, everything is pretty clear. Thanks."

Kennedy turned to Darius, a cha-cha dance happening in the pit of her stomach. There was no preventing what eye contact with him did to her. At least no one could see what was happening in her chest cavity. "And what about you, Darius? Questions or concerns that I need to handle?"

"I'm good for now, but I won't hesitate to reach out when I do. I think we're all about ready for lunch now. Sound good?"

"Yes, I'm starved." She turned to Mike. "Thanks for the walkthrough, Mike. We're going to head to lunch now. Sure you don't want to come?" *Please come.*

"Nah. I'll stick around here for a while and grab something on my way back into town. I'll give you a call later."

"Okay. See you later." Kennedy turned her attention to the group, careful not to lock eyes with Darius. "You guys can follow me. The restaurant is about twenty minutes out."

Darius bowed his head and extended his hand forward. "After you."

Nina shuffled toward Kennedy's side. "Mind if I hitch a ride with you, Kennedy?"

"Of course not. I'd be honored to have *the* Nina McCall ride along with me. Come."

Kennedy and Nina strolled ahead while Mike lagged behind and talked with the McCall men on the quarter-mile walk back to their cars. They didn't speak much to keep from having to raise their voices over the construction work. When they arrived back at Kennedy's car and strapped their seatbelts, Nina flashed one of those smiles a woman would give to an old girlfriend when she wanted juicy details.

Nina had some sort of plan up her sleeve, and something told Kennedy it had everything to do with Darius. She adored Nina and the encouragement she often dished out, but Kennedy refused to be on the receiving end of relational advice she didn't even ask for.

Now probably wasn't a good time to find a polite way to send her back to her family's car. This was going to be one long drive if Nina brought up the one thing she tried

to keep her mind off—any personal dealings with Darius

McCall.

# Eight

Nina made small talk as Kennedy navigated along the farm-to-market roads and finally to Interstate 10, where traffic was at a standstill. *Great.* Kennedy semi-held her breath waiting for Nina to reveal the real reason behind that sheepish smile she'd given earlier. If she leaned on her intuition, she would bet that Nina wasn't as interested about where she grew up and what she liked to do around town as much as she was interested about her love life.

"So, Kennedy, are you and my brother-in-law a thing?" Nina's eyebrows danced, and that same smile she had earlier returned.

Boom. There it was.

"No, ma'am. Business associates is all. What made you ask me that?" It had to be that little fiasco of her gawking at his ring finger that morning.

Nina looked down and rubbed her protruding belly. "It's pretty obvious you two like each other, but looks like you're fighting it for some silly reason."

Silly? Her reasoning was justified.

Kennedy peeled her eyes away from the car's bumper in front of her and searched Nina's eyes. How serious was she? Or was this that thing people did where they poked around for information? "I don't know what you're talking about."

"Kennedy, you've been feeding yourself that lie for so long you believe it. No one is in the car with us, so it's okay to say you like him. He's not bad to look at, so no woman with eyes would blame you."

Kennedy threw her head back against the headrest and silently bemoaned the fact that traffic was moving five miles per hour, which left plenty of time for her and Nina to have this unwanted conversation. Though it was halfway nice to have someone to talk to about this war going on within her. She'd practically pushed the few friends she had left away when her brother died and secluded herself from the world, with the exception of her aunt Mabel and Mike.

"We work together, so if we were attracted to each other, we couldn't do anything about it."

Nina waved her off. "*Pssh.* Honey, looks like we've got plenty of time, so I'm going to share my story with you.

Andrew and I dated in college and broke up shortly after graduation because we wanted two different things. And to be honest with you, that was the biggest relationship mistake I made. I regretted it for a long time and probably wouldn't have done anything about it if I weren't diagnosed with a terminal illness toward the end of last year."

Kennedy clutched her chest and gasped.

Nina threw her palm in the air in a stop motion. "Hold on. I'm not done. The doctors told me I had thirty days to live. Thirty. Can you imagine what that feels like? Knowing the expiration date on your life? It was scary, but I knew I didn't want to go to my grave with the only man I ever truly loved not knowing I still loved him. Now the circumstances were pretty messed up, and initially he wouldn't budge, but when I shared those facts with him, he decided that he wanted to spend that time with me, too. You can take my advice with a grain of salt, but I shared my story

to say not to let something like work get in between you two.

If you're interested, give it a shot. It may work out or it may

not, but at least your conscience will be clear in knowing that

you did at least try."

"Wow. What happened with your diagnosis?"

"Turns out it was a benign tumor, and I'm still here

four months later carrying this little bug."

"What a testimony."

"I know, right? But I'm convinced that God allows

things to happen like that sometimes to give us the kick in

the rear end we need. For me, that drew me closer to God

and sent me straight into the arms of the man I love. Though

it was a scary time, I wouldn't take any of it back because

I'm at peace with where I am right now. It had to happen. So

that brings us to you, Kennedy. You'll have to decide what

you want. We miss one hundred percent of the shots we never take."

Kennedy heaved a sigh and gripped the steering wheel. That was so easy to say because Nina wasn't in her shoes. No doubt she had a terrible but life-altering experience, and it was nice that things worked out for her. However, dating Darius could affect her livelihood and their business if it didn't work out.

In a faint voice, almost as if she were talking to herself, Kennedy asked, "Do you think it's even possible for Darius and me to date and work with each other?"

"Possible if that's what you two want."

"He's never said dating is what he wants. Never even hinted at it. I'm not sure he's interested."

Nina leaned forward, flipped down the sun visor in front of Kennedy, and opened the attached mirror. "Honey,

..t here." Nina tapped on the mirror. "You're gorgeous. Darius can see that. In fact, I believe that's why he was trippin' over the fact that a woman is in charge of SCI—and not just any woman, a beautiful woman. Oh, he's interested alright, but like you, he has a lot at stake and doesn't want to mess this project up in any kind of way. The poor man's eyes and mind are superglued on becoming CEO. If you ask me, he could use a beautiful distraction." Nina winked.

Traffic slightly picked up, and Kennedy drove at forty miles per hour as opposed to the five she'd been doing for the last twenty minutes. "You're funny, and I like you, but I think it's best if Darius and I keep things the way they are for now."

"I like you, too, and I think you'd make a great sister-in-law. Just think about what I said. Time can be our friend or our enemy."

It was almost as if Nina controlled the traffic, because as soon as she finished with her speech, the lanes opened, and they traveled at sixty-five miles per hour. Thankfully, their heart-to-heart was over, though appreciated. They spent the rest of the time talking about Nina's career as a motivational speaker and then Kennedy's start as the president of SCI. Nina was easy to talk to, almost like a sister. A sister who seemed to have been planted in the car with her to put her matchmaking skills to use.

Too bad Nina's story wasn't enough to convince her to see Darius outside of work.

∞

"What've you been doing out here for entertainment, bro?"

Darius, despising the question, glanced up to see Andrew's smirk in the rearview mirror and brushed him off with a snort. "Work. Gotta stay ahead of the game." Darius turned the volume up on the radio.

"Staying ahead of the game, as you put it, is all good, but take time to relax, son. Enjoy the city. The entire experience can be helpful with marketing. Get to know the area. You have Kennedy as a resource. I'm sure she can help."

"Dad, I try to keep my distance from Kennedy unless it's related to this project. She has a job to do, and so do I." That came out fast and wrong. Too late to take back.

Andrew slid to the edge of his seat. "What did you do?"

"Why do you always assume the worst about me?"

"I didn't say anything. I asked a question. Why are you so defensive?"

"I'm not defensive, but it seems you have a problem with and question everything I do. I'm here to do a job, that's it."

"Oh, I see. You asked her out on a date, and she turned you down."

"Man, whatever. I'm not even going to dignify you with a response."

Jeffrey piped in. "Well, I want one. Did anything happen between you two? Are you causing trouble? Didn't we talk about this?"

"What's with the twenty questions? We are not dating." Darius emphasized every syllable. "I didn't think I had to verbalize for the thousandth time how important this project is to me. I'm focused enough not to get distracted."

"Distraction could be good for you, bro. I'm not saying it has to be Kennedy—in fact, I'd prefer that it isn't. But what I'm saying is that you need to lighten up a bit and have some fun. Houston is filled with beautiful women. Shoot, I'm pretty sure Nina knows someone she can link you up with. I trust her judgment."

That woman could tell him the sky was purple and that it was raining lemon drops and he'd believe it. If there was a man he didn't want to be like, it was his older brother. Look at what love had done to him. Andrew had grown soft, practically eating up Nina's every word. Asking her advice before he made any decisions. Catering to her every need. Putty. That's what Andrew had become, and if love had a way of doing that to a man—a McCall man at that—he'd steer clear of it. A casual date here and there was fine, but nothing that could become serious. And every fiber of his being screamed serious whenever he looked into Kennedy's eyes.

That was his problem.

If he could manage his emotions around her, then he'd be all for a date with her on occasion.

"I can find my own date when I have time for one. Thank you."

"Alright. Don't say I didn't try to help."

"If I need your help, I'll ask for it."

"Well, you need to do something because this attitude of yours is getting old, son. Drew is just concerned about you. Your mother and I are, too, so don't bite his head off. Good you're focused on this project and we're off to a great start, but work can't be the only thing filling your life. You need something else."

"And what might that be?" Darius almost regretted he asked.

"I can't tell you that. It's something you'll have to figure out for yourself. I just don't want my son working himself into an early grave. Live a little."

The first ten minutes of their bumper-to-bumper ride had been filled with comfortable silence aside from the R&B music playing through the thirteen-speaker radio system. And suddenly Andrew sneakily brought up his love life. For the life of him, he could only pray that Nina wasn't in the car ahead attempting to fix him up with Kennedy. But something told him that was a prayer that would go unanswered. In fact, all of this was probably a setup and Nina's idea, which circled back to the fact that she had Andrew lapping out the palm of her hand.

"Alright. We're here." Darius navigated into a parking space directly behind Kennedy and watched her and Nina for a minute before he cut the engine and climbed out of the car. They smiled and laughed like old girlfriends with Nina invading Kennedy's personal space, her hand resting on her shoulder as they shared what seemed to be a funny joke. The way Kennedy's hair fell over her shoulders when she threw her head back said she enjoyed the drive with Nina and found whatever she'd just said amusing.

Secretly, he was jealous of Nina in that moment.

She could laugh and talk with Kennedy without worrying about work or what other people would think. She could just be. And why did he want that freedom with Kennedy, too?

Andrew strode to his wife's side, and Darius watched her whisper something in his ear, to which he smiled and glanced over his shoulder at Darius, a smirk tugging at the corners of his lips. Andrew obviously wanted him to know they were talking about him, but he didn't care. He could bet money on the subject, too.

Darius and Jeffrey joined the trio, and one look into Kennedy's eyes told him that Nina planted seeds in her head, too.

Seeds he wished he could water.

Seeds he wished could grow into something beautiful, except his brother had been proof that emotions couldn't be trusted.

# Nine

Kennedy and Nina were becoming fast friends.

Somehow Nina had gotten her to open up and let her imaginary emotional guard down. They'd talked or texted at least four times a week since Nina's visit two weeks ago. The sister-like bond was welcomed by Kennedy, especially since she'd lost the only sibling she had. It was Nina who attempted to convince Kennedy to take Darius to the painting class later that week she'd signed up for, but against that advice, she invited her aunt Mabel instead.

It was best that way.

After a day of endless calls, Kennedy could only think about spending the evening at Paint Until You Faint and sharing some quality time with her aunt Mabel. Nowadays they hardly ever saw each other outside of work.

Kennedy stuffed her tote with her laptop and the Doberman project file. Her head jerked up at the sound of two light taps on her office door. Mabel poked her head inside but didn't come in.

"Hey. Are you ready? I was just packing up."

"Actually," she said, clearing her throat and massaging her chest, "I think I should just go home and lie down. I'm so sorry to have to cancel on you. Do you want me to check if Mike can go in my place?"

Kennedy's shoulders slumped and the corners of her lips turned down. "No. I already know Mike can't go. With daylight savings time in full effect, they're working longer hours on the McCall project. He'll be too late getting back to town to go with me." Kennedy waved it off. "It's okay. I don't mind going by myself."

"How about you take Mr. McCall with you? I'm not suggesting a date, but it could be an opportunity for you to talk about the project in a casual atmosphere. And who knows? Maybe it'll spark something within him to add such an activity to the lineup for the guests to enjoy at the new resort."

Kennedy thought for a moment and hesitated before answering. Everything Mabel said sounded a lot like something Nina would say. She searched Mabel's eyes for any hint of cahoots with Nina, but that had to be silly because Nina wouldn't take it that far. "That's one way to look at it. I'll give him a call to see if he's available."

"If it'll ease your worries and help this to feel less like a date, I can call to make arrangements. I'm the office receptionist after all. It's what I'm here for."

"No. That's okay. I'll reach out to him."

Mabel backed out of the office with one of those if-you-say-so looks. It couldn't hurt to ask, though she halfway hoped he would be busy—the chicken's way out of saying she tried and could move on.

Kennedy dialed Darius from the office phone, and he answered before the line completed the first full ring.

"Hey. It's Kennedy Slaughter from SCI."

"Kennedy, I know who you are. No need to sound so formal. Is there a problem?"

"No. The project is fine. I'm calling because I have an extra ticket to a painting event tonight and wanted to see if you're available to come with me. Mabel was supposed to come, but she isn't feeling very well. It's BYOB—bring your own bottle—except I don't drink, so I'll stop by Sonic on my way to buy a Route 44 slush. You can take whatever you want if you want to come along."

That was way more information than he needed to make an informed decision. If she wasn't asking him out on a date, it surely felt like it, with the receiver sliding around her palm and her heart galloping at the rate of horse's hooves.

"That sounds interesting. Count me in. Name the time and place."

"Two hours. I'll text you the address."

"I'll pick you up, and we can go together, if that's okay."

*Do I want to be confined in a car with Darius?*

Maybe she was the one making too much out of this. Not once had he implied he was interested in her, and she was confident enough that her reasons for asking him to attend were clear. He was her last resort, and she didn't mind going alone if she had to, so this was a friendly, casual outing.

*Don't make this more than what it is.*

"That's fine, but you'll need to come an hour ahead of time so we have time to pick up drinks and arrive a few minutes early."

"I can live with that. Text me your address, and I'll see you in an hour."

"See you then."

Kennedy grabbed her tote, phone, and keys and hustled out of her office through the lobby, only to be stopped by a wide-mouthed Mabel. "Was Darius available?"

"Yes, he is. He's gonna pick me up in an hour, so I need to run home, freshen up, and change. I thought you were on your way out, too."

Mabel waved her off. "Oh, I'm right behind you. I just need to make a quick call. Go on. Don't want you to run into traffic and be late for your date—I mean your business meeting. You know the difference a couple of minutes makes with this Houston traffic."

"I hear ya. I'll see you Monday."

∞

Kennedy's invitation came right after Darius had finished his midday workout. Next on his agenda was a shower and more work. Her invitation served as a reminder of his brother's and father's advice to enjoy something other than business. As always, he'd put in more than enough effort for McCall Resorts today, probably enough to carry him through the next week if he didn't open his laptop again until the following Friday.

He stood under the showerhead and allowed the pounding of the water droplets against his skin to ease his aching muscles, compliments of the weight training he'd taken up since arriving in Houston. He replayed the conversation he'd had with Kennedy minutes ago, and he couldn't help but chuckle. She made sure he knew this was not a date and that she'd only asked him because she had no one else to take on such short notice. Under ordinary circumstances, he'd be offended that he was last on her list, but given he didn't have any companions in town, and he found her attractive, he accepted the invitation.

Personal or not, he'd consider himself a fool for turning down an invitation from her on a Friday evening.

Though a relationship was off limits, there were no rules that stated the two of them couldn't be friends.

He cranked off the water, toweled off, and dressed in khakis and an ocean blue short-sleeved polo shirt. After grooming himself, he scooped his keys off the counter and strode to his car. It was as if his family could sniff out his movement. Before he had the chance to input Kennedy's address into the GPS, a call from his mother came through the car's Bluetooth.

"What's going on, Ma?" He thought twice about answering, but if he didn't, calls would stream through from his father and brother soon to reach him on her behalf, especially since he hadn't talked to her since Sunday. Normally, he'd speak with her at least twice during the week, but he'd been caught up in work for the past few days, moreso than usual.

"Oh, not much—same old, same old around here. What are you doing on this Friday night?"

"Kennedy and I are having sort of a business discussion in about an hour."

"It's eight o'clock here, and we're an hour ahead. You mean to tell me y'all are having a business discussion at eight o'clock on a Friday night? Where is this meeting taking place?"

"It's casual. We're gonna paint at this place called Paint Until You Faint."

"Oh, I see. You mean a date?"

"No, Ma. You know I wouldn't get involved with her like that while we're in the middle of this project. We've gotta keep our heads. Besides, it really isn't anything like that, so don't make a big deal about it."

"I completely understand." He didn't get the feeling she did given the smile that could be heard in her voice.

He could hear Nina's voice in the background but couldn't make out what she was saying. The only word he heard clearly was Kennedy's name.

"Okay, Ma. I'll catch up with you tomorrow."

"Have fun and enjoy your non-date."

Darius pressed the button on the steering wheel to end the call, input Kennedy's address into the navigation system, and set course for her place. He shook his head to rid himself of his mother's final words. That woman would do whatever she could if it meant getting him a step closer to a committed relationship. As long as he and Kennedy were on the same page, it was all good.

Twenty-five minutes later, he pulled into the driveway of Kennedy's brick one-story home. The simple, yet clean landscaping with knock-out rosebushes reminded him of her—beautiful, but she didn't have to go out of her way to show it. It was just who she was.

Darius tapped a rhythmical seven beats on her door. She appeared shortly after with her hair pulled into a ponytail, dressed in one of those one-piece outfits women called rompers.

Breathtaking.

And although this wasn't a date, he felt like he should've shown up with flowers or something. He made a mental note to do so if there was a next time. Even friends gave friends flowers.

"Hey, you're on time. Let me grab my purse and keys."

"I'll wait for you right here."

Kennedy reappeared a minute later wearing a full-faced smile and shimmied her shoulders. "You ready to paint until you faint?"

"I guess we'll see. I'm no good at painting though, so don't hold that against me."

"Me either, but it's fun, and they show you exactly what to do. Quite relaxing, too. You'll see." Kennedy locked the door and followed Darius to the car where he opened the door like the perfect gentleman.

Once Kennedy was safely inside, Darius shuffled around to the driver's side and climbed in behind the wheel. "Let's get you to Sonic for that drink. I'll just grab a lemonade from there as well, though nothing can beat the fresh peach lemonades we serve at the resort back in Georgia, so that will have to do."

From memory, Darius drove to the Sonic drive-thru he'd passed on the way to her house, about two miles down the road. The timing proved perfect because after ordering and arriving at the painting place, they had just enough time to grab supplies and find seats.

Easels and white canvases with the outline of the night's picture were positioned in front of every seat in the room. Darius and Kennedy sat on the front row and settled onto their stools.

"Oh, I can trace with the skill of a third grader. I think I got this."

Kennedy chuckled. "You sure? Look there." She pointed to a display painting in front of the room. "That is what your picture should look like when you're done."

"Didn't you say that they'll give us instructions?"

"Yeah. Why?"

"Because I'm pretty good at following directions, too. I'm sure mine will look better than anyone else's."

"That's a pretty cocky attitude for someone who's never done this before. Care to bet on it—at least that yours will look better than mine by the end of the night?"

"What's the wager?"

"Loser buys lunch."

Sure, they were just jiving around, but he'd buy her lunch any day, bet or no bet, yet he agreed. "You're on. Don't go cryin' and coming up with excuses. I want all of my winnings. And I like to eat, too, so I'm not picking a sandwich shop. I'm thinking shrimp, steak, lobster sort of lunch."

"Sounds more like dinner to me."

"Are you offering?"

"In your dreams. Put your game face on because it's about to go down." Kennedy squinted and pursed her lips in mock seriousness. An innocent move on her part, but the sheen from her lips drew his eyes to them. His thoughts betrayed him, and all he could think about was if her lip gloss had any flavor.

"Good evening. I'm Sharon, and I'll be your host for this evening. Everyone have their drinks, their brushes, and their paints?"

Thank goodness for Sharon.

Sharon stood next to the painting at the front of the room, but also had an outlined canvas like the participants. "We're gonna take this step by step. First paint all the stems by brushing along the outline like this," she said and demonstrated.

"So, is this something you like to do in addition to the yoga and meditation you mentioned?"

"Yes. This is one activity that relaxes me. Work can be stressful sometimes with employees counting on me to make the right decisions. What about you?"

"I'm a runner. It's about the only thing I make time for other than work. It's strenuous exercise, but I always feel better and have a greater sense of clarity when the run is over."

"Ah, running is torture. Do you have a special place you like to run back at home?"

"I do. I've sort of created my own path near the main house. I can't wait for you to see it in person, I mean when everything is built out here."

"Trust me, I'm looking forward to it. Everything about it seems magical, like something we'd experience out of the country, or at the very least, outside the state of Texas."

Sharon interrupted their conversation and introduced the next step. They half-listened and kept their attention on each other.

Darius hadn't had the opportunity before now to sit as close to her, but welcomed the nearness. Her eyes were what he would describe as brown with flecks of gold. Or he could have been trippin' and the flecks were actually from the light in the room. Whatever the case, they pulled him in and made it hard for him to focus on the painting or anything else happening around him.

"That's part of what makes McCall resorts unique—we want our guests to experience magic, romance, rejuvenation without having to travel halfway across the world."

"What are your plans once we're finished here? You plan to stick around and manage the Houston resort or go back to Georgia?"

By this time, Darius had abandoned his painting and swiveled on his barstool to face her. "Honestly, I'm in limbo. I've always seen myself running the company in Georgia, but there's no reason I couldn't do that from here. Here or there, I'd have to travel frequently—at least until we're fully established, and the resort is functioning here like the resort in Georgia. And that decision isn't solely mine to make, though I don't foresee my dad or Andrew having an issue if I wanted to stay. My goal is to do what's best for McCall Resorts."

Kennedy nodded as if she understood. "The good thing about all that is you have people to lean on, and you don't have to go it alone. With SCI, I have to run it. Kendrick and I didn't have any other siblings, and our parents are gone, too. It's just me, so even if I wanted to do something else with my life, I couldn't."

Darius brushed his knuckle under her chin and lifted her head to meet his eyes. "Is there something else you want to do with your life?"

"Yeah, but that was a long time ago, and I'm too old for it now."

"Tell me. I won't judge. Just a friend who was invited out as a last resort because you had no one else to call."

They burst into laughter and quickly sobered when they garnered the attention of the patrons surrounding them.

"I knew that would come up eventually. But to be honest, I would have asked you first if I thought you were interested in coming, but with us working together, I didn't want to blur the lines, you know?"

"I'm with you. I understand." Darius held her gaze for a moment before asking, "Now about this dream…"

"Dance. I used to dance, but because of an accident, I had to give that up. Once I'd gotten over it, I decided I would open my own dance studio and give dance lessons in jazz, tap, ballet, and hip-hop."

The light in her eyes was unmistakable, and not from the overhead lights. Those flecks of gold were there and illuminated all the more when she discussed her dream.

"And how'd you end up here?"

"This was only supposed to be temporary, working with Kendrick and keeping his books, but the company grew fast, which forced me to learn more about the industry. Don't get me wrong: I like it, and I would do anything for my brother, just didn't think I'd be around ten years later and in his place."

Darius drummed up several solutions to her problem, all of which she'd probably curse him for even bringing them up, so he kept them to himself. What was it about her that made him want to fix this for her, to give her the best of both worlds when it wasn't his place or his business to do so?

"I have a feeling you'll be able to do everything you've dreamed of one day. Just don't lose hope, and don't bury your dreams."

Who was he? And why did he sound like he'd been listening to Nina talk for too long?

"Thanks, Darius. Let's finish up. You can spend about two hours encouraging me not to give up over this lunch you're gonna owe me at the end of the night."

Kennedy bamboozled him.

Had she known he'd be so caught up in her that he'd neglect his painting? Darius would happily forfeit, but he had to show that he put forth an honest effort. He spent the next thirty minutes doing so, though a rush job. At the end, he presented C-plus work at best compared to Kennedy's B-plus, which earned her a free lunch. And she wasn't shy about rubbing it in his face either, with taking pictures using her cell phone of both their paintings to commemorate the moment.

This entire evening shrunk his resolve.

He shouldn't have asked her such personal questions because the more he knew about her, the less he wanted to be only friends. Knowing her heart botched his plans to keep this evening on a non-date level. He wasn't a pro at dating, but this was definitely a real date, no matter if they tagged it as such or not.

The problem as he saw it was how to maintain a balance of whatever this was and business, because he enjoyed her company and wanted more of it.

# Ten

Winning the bet catapulted Kennedy and Darius into a lunch routine.

And no matter how much she internally denied it, they were practically dating. For two weekends in a row, combined with three days during the week, Darius had become her lunch partner. They'd somehow fallen into this natural rhythm of calling each other and scheduling time to try new restaurants.

It became their thing.

Eat something new and discuss business. Well business was what they used as an excuse because more times than not, the McCall project often fell to the bottom of their list of discussion topics. Everything that needed to be said took place during their weekly meeting updates.

Kennedy stared blankly at her computer screen, seeing but not paying attention. Her phone rang, jolting her from the haze, and her heart sank a little when Nina's name lit the screen.

"I hope you're free for lunch tomorrow."

Tomorrow would cut into a day she'd hoped to dine with her newest friend, Darius. "Why? What's up?"

"Drew and I are coming to town for the closing on the sale of my house. It was supposed to be next week, but got bumped up to tomorrow. You free?"

"Should be."

"To be completely honest, Darius will be there, too, but I promise this isn't an attempt to set you up. We're only in town for a brief stint and wanted to make sure we poked our heads in to say hi and to give Drew an opportunity to follow up on project progress."

"No need to explain. It's all good. My meeting schedule is open for tomorrow, so just let me know when you guys are ready."

Nina and Andrew's presence at their next lunch outing could be a good thing—to keep her emotions in check.

"Will do," Nina answered before she ended the call.

Kennedy found her unbelievable. Even though she said including her in their family lunch wasn't a matchmaking attempt, Kennedy perceived it as such. Nina had taken every opportunity to remind her that tomorrow isn't promised and that she owed it to herself to see if her attraction to Darius was worth exploring.

But she was fine with the way things were now— good company and good food. No expectations and no distractions from what was most important to both of them— getting the job done right.

Her screen hadn't rested long enough to return to sleep mode before Darius' phone call came through.

"Hey, I was hoping we could try The Catch tomorrow, but Drew and Nina will be in town. You game today? What's your workday look like?"

Kennedy sucked the air between her teeth and released an uncertain breath. "Sounds good, but I don't want to come back into the office smelling like fried fish."

"Would you rather we have a late lunch/early dinner? I can power through lunch and wait until the end of the day if you like that idea better."

"Ooh yes, that sounds good. I hate to have to turn down shrimp." She chuckled. "I'll call when I'm leaving the office, and we can meet at the Post Oak location."

A contradictory sense of relief washed over her when they ended their call. The mere fact that her heart beat double time and her chest expanded when Darius rearranged their outing from lunch to dinner told her she was headed for trouble. That sort of excitement happened between people who were officially dating, not between friends slash business associates. Her common, rational business sense urged her to take a step back and come up with an excuse to cancel, but that tiny organ slightly left of the center in her chest wanted more time with him, to get to know him and witness the contagious joy when he spoke about his plans for the new resort.

*I can put an end to this if things get out of hand.*

But for now, the Doberman project was in post-construction phase, and the final document review called her name. As the superintendent, Mike had taken care of the punch list, certificate of substantial completion, inspection certificates, certificate of occupancy, and all other paperwork. She just had to review and sign off, which summed her to-do list for the remainder of the afternoon.

Enough work to keep her mind from thoughts of her early evening visit with Darius.

∞

"Speak your mind, Drew. You look constipated."

Andrew coughed, massaged his chest, then chugged a glass of water.

Up until then, Nina and Kennedy carried the conversation between the four of them. Through appetizers and halfway through lunch, Andrew hadn't talked much, which put Darius on high alert. Either something was wrong at work or with their parents, both of which dried his palate, no matter how many glasses of water he finished.

"I'm not sure now is the time to have this conversation." Andrew darted his eyes in Kennedy's direction before bouncing back to Darius.

"Whatever it is, it has you more uptight than usual, so let's hear it. What's going on?"

Nina squeezed Andrew's shoulder and nodded in encouragement.

*Is he dying now?*

"I know how much being CEO means to you, and in previous conversations, we discussed me returning to

Jackson State to teach, but I've—well, we've—come to a different decision. I'm keeping the job. Teaching is something I believe I—"

"What the—" Darius dropped his fork on the half-empty plate, remembered Kennedy sat next to him, and bit his tongue. It mattered what she thought about him. Why? He knew but couldn't acknowledge the reasoning, especially not now, after his brother vexed his spirit.

"Just hear me out first. I like the job a lot more than I thought I would. Maybe we can come to some sort of an arrangement where we both get what we want."

"First, we couldn't get you to come home, and now you don't wanna leave? How did I know this would happen?"

"Stop making this about you, Darius."

"What do you mean not make this about me? This has everything to do with me. You flew all the way out here to tell me that. You could've sent an e-mail to spell out how you planned to stab me in the back."

"You know it's not like that, bro."

"Bro? How can you call me brother after you just sat here and disrespected me like that? That wasn't the deal, Drew, and you know it. I'm out." Darius stood and tossed a couple of twenty-dollar bills on the table. "Kennedy, I'm sorry they dragged you here as a buffer. I'll be in touch—unless Drew plans to come here and take over this project as well."

Darius spun on his heel to leave, but did an about-face. "Is that your plan, too? To come out here, run the project, and take credit for something you didn't do?"

Andrew stood and attempted to calm Darius—the bass in his voice drawing stares from other patrons.

"Nah, I'm good. Finish your food and take care of your wife."

Kennedy apologized to Nina, excused herself from the table, and shuffled behind Darius. She didn't offer apologies or attempt to convince him to rejoin his brother at the table. Instead, she linked her hand in his and his steps slowed, but he continued along his determined path to his car. The comfort from her touch said more than any word she could've uttered. And despite the anger that burned within him, that unaddressed connection they shared, that fire that burned within his heart that usually made it speed up, now slowed down, and calmed him.

And that made him even more upset because he was in the middle of a fight with his brother who had derailed his goals.

And she touched him.

And his heart succumbed to her warmth and comfort.

At the pace he stormed away from the table, he could've made it to his car in one minute. But because of Kennedy, the walk took more like five minutes.

"Thank you," Darius said when they made it to his car.

"You're welcome. Figured you could use a friend right now."

"You figured right." On instinct, he pulled her into the comfort of his arms—well, more like he rested in the solace of her embrace. He had to be twice her size, and still her arms wrapped around him, provided everything he needed, like refuge in the midst of a storm. And she didn't let go. She held on for as long as he did until he peeled her hands from his waist, held them securely in his, and squeezed.

Her eyes twinkled with understanding. He didn't have to tell her what a blow Andrew had delivered because he'd talked with her about his plans for when he became CEO on several occasions. In fact, at almost every opportunity, she indulged him. Her lips called to him, and his vulnerability wanted to take over. Kissing her would also make him feel better, but whenever they shared their first kiss, he didn't want it to be because his emotions were all over the place. There couldn't be any doubt in her mind what that kiss meant, so he restrained himself.

Their time would come.

He caught wind of Andrew and Nina in his peripheral vision, and his heartrate escalated at the same level as if he were on a rollercoaster. He couldn't stomach more of Andrew right now, so he escorted Kennedy to her car where she'd parked three spaces down, relished in the comfort of her embrace one last time, opened her car door, and saw her off.

Darius didn't give Andrew enough time to apologize or talk things out. He climbed into his own car and raced out of the parking lot with one thought on his mind: talking to his father.

Why hadn't his father mentioned Andrew's newfound desire to stay?

How long ago had Andrew made this decision?

And what did Andrew's decision mean for his future at McCall Resorts?

# Eleven

When Darius invited Kennedy to travel alongside him back to his family's resort in Georgia to experience the resort first-hand as his special guest, but mostly to be his support system while he went to meet with his father to discuss his future at McCall Resorts, she didn't think they'd be on a first-class flight within a week's time.

Instinct whispered to stay as far away from Darius and his family as possible, especially with this rift between Darius and his brother. But curiosity and the plain-ole need to do something for herself—live spontaneously—shouted louder, and she agreed. Besides, Mabel and Mike knew how to reach her if necessary, and the trip would only last a couple of days.

They'd been wheels up in the air for ten minutes, and Kennedy worked her jaw to release her plugged ears. Chewing gum didn't help as it had in the past.

Darius nudged her elbow. "Hey, you all good? Need anything?"

"I'm good for now. You?" Kennedy searched his eyes to listen beyond his words. The worry lines in his forehead had multiplied since their lunch with Andrew and Nina last week. He tried to hide his lack of sleep behind his toothy smile, but the dark circles under his eyes gave him away. If only a hand squeeze would ease his anxiety, she'd do it, but the poor man was close to losing it.

"Yeah. Thanks for coming to check out the resort. I appreciate the support you've given to me. It means a lot."

"No problem. You had me at spa. If you need me at all this weekend, that's where you'll find me."

Darius took hold of her hand in his and caressed her knuckles. The heat from their shared touch warmed her entire arm followed by an unfamiliar tingling sensation. Her eyes dipped down to his touch then back up to his smoldering orbs. "You deserve it, especially after putting up with me these last few months."

"You ain't never lied 'bout that."

They shared a laugh, and Darius squeezed her hand to reiterate his point, and her heart cosigned. *Don't let go.*

"Thank you for being a friend, Kennedy. And speaking of friend, I wouldn't be a good one if I didn't make sure you spent a little time in the barre classes."

"Shut up! How did I not know about that?"

Darius teased. "Seems to me you slacked on your homework."

Perfect time to slide her hand out of his to tag him, but Kennedy didn't want to be the first one to break their connection. A connection that somehow solidified when she comforted him days ago by slipping her hand in his. That lunch didn't turn out anything like she'd expected. Had Nina been trying to use her to soften the blow? Had all the phone calls and texts been prep work for when the time came for Andrew to break the news to Darius? Kennedy fought the urge to believe that Nina would use her in that way and refused to believe the thoughts rounding up in her head about her new friend until she had proof.

"This is going to be a nice trip, and don't you worry either. I know I've only met your father a few times, but from what I gather, he is a man of his word. And while we're on the topic, I'm going to throw in my two cents." She squeezed his hand tighter this time and held his gaze. "Figure out a way to work this out with your brother. He won't always be around, and I'd hate for you to live with regrets about your relationship. I don't want that for you."

"Thanks."

And just like that, she lost him. The warmth in his eyes dissipated, replaced with a blank stare. The softness and light were gone. His grip loosened, but he didn't let go of her hand. Forgiving his brother and looking for a solution was not what Darius had in mind, but she hoped she could help him see the situation in a different light.

This weekend just might turn out to be longer than she thought—and not in a good sort of way.

Kennedy shifted and rested against her wide, plush seat, closed her eyes, and prayed for Darius and his family.

*Father God, You know how all this ends and what needs to take place here. Help me to be the friend Darius needs, and give him the capacity to love bigger and to see this through Your lens. Your thoughts are not our thoughts, and Your ways are not our ways. I'm thankful for that. Guide us along the path You have destined for us this weekend and every day after. In Jesus' name. Amen.*

∞

He'd gone out on a limb when he'd asked Kennedy to accompany him back to Georgia under the guise of business and for her to experience the resort as his guest. That was practically an offer she couldn't refuse. But in truth, they'd spent the last few weekends together, and he didn't want to be without her this weekend either, especially with the insurmountable stress he faced with McCall Resorts leadership. However, that was one truth he couldn't share with her or anyone else. And besides, he hadn't quite accepted it either—that he looked forward to spending time with her, that her presence was the period to his day.

Darius navigated down the winding road to the McCall estate. Miles of green acreage at one time brought him peace. Trepidation tore through his core, but the reassuring smile on Kennedy's lips calmed him. He halfway regretted bringing her in the middle of his family affairs, but the selfish part of him just wanted her.

Kennedy gasped, and her mouth hung open. "This is your family's estate? Are you like the prince of Zamunda or something? Have any secrets you want to share before we arrive in the next few minutes?"

Darius threw his head back and chuckled. He needed that laugh. "Nah, far from it. This all started when my grandfather left my dad the farmland, and it's grown exponentially over the years. I don't even think my father knew that it would come to this."

"The online pictures don't do this place any justice." Kennedy leaned forward and braced the dashboard, nearly spraining her neck to take in the lush green scenery, farmland, and buildings that looked like they could be mini castles. "I'm tempted to request that you just leave me here."

Darius chuckled again, refreshed by her excitement. "You haven't had the chance to do anything just yet."

"This here is a picture from my dreams. Gorgeous. Southeast Texas is not prepared for what they're gonna get."

"Well, I can certainly appreciate that. There really is nothing like getting a chance to see and experience this place for yourself." Darius pulled into the circular driveway and parked. "Your room is ready, but I figured you may want to holler at Nina before you get settled. This is the main house where my family lives. We have our own living quarters, sort of like an apartment within the house."

"First of all, if you used the term *living quarters*, that means you live in a mansion. No need to be shy about it, prince of Zamunda. This here," she said, pointing to the house, "is the very definition of a mansion. Can I have a tour?"

"Of course. I don't mind showing you around, but first I should warn you…" Darius shifted in his seat toward Kennedy. "My mom may get the wrong idea with me bringing you here. You and I know there's nothing between us and that we're just friends…" Everything within him screamed *liar* as the words filtered through his lips, and even his stomach and heart wrenched in protest. "But she may not see it that way, so if she gets a little pushy, it's okay to be firm with her."

Kennedy covered his hand with hers. "Seriously, Darius, I think you're worried for nothing. About everything. It'll all work out. I believe that, and you should, too." She gave his hands one of those pats people gave to kids after a pep talk. Only he was far from a child, and any touch from her encouraged parts of him that should in fact be discouraged. They'd already put each other in the friend zone. Being a good friend was the whole reason she was there with him in the first place.

Right?

"Alright, Miss Slaughter. I've done all I can to warn you." Darius shook his head and shot her a you'll-see-for-yourself glance before climbing out of the car and shuffling around to the passenger side to get the door for her.

Squared shoulders, puffed chest, with an indignant lift of his chin, Darius was poised for a fight when he crossed the threshold through the double-door entrance with Kennedy at his side. But the first face he saw softened his demeanor with a warm smile.

"Mom, you good?" Darius wrapped her in an embrace, which was shorter than he intended it to be. She broke free of his embrace and stepped to the side, her eyes settling on Kennedy, a wider-than-life smile graced her lips.

"You must be Miss Kennedy Slaughter. I'm Rose McCall, Darius' mother and creator and editor of *The Peach Buzz,* McCall Resorts biannual magazine." Rose McCall encircled both of her hands around Kennedy's.

"Nice to meet you, Mrs. McCall. This place is amazing." Kennedy's gaze darted around the foyer.

"Oh, come for a tour." Rose extended her elbow and Kennedy accepted, allowing Rose to whisk her away.

"I was planning to do that," Darius said to no one in particular because the two had already left him standing in the foyer.

With Kennedy occupied for a while, Darius took the free time as an opportunity to get the conversation started with his dad regarding Andrew's little announcement. He strode through the hall to his father's office where he expected to find him on a Friday afternoon. Jeffrey McCall usually worked in the office on Friday mornings and worked from home after lunch, unless he had a scheduled meeting, which he did his best to avoid on Fridays.

Darius double tapped on the half-opened sliding door frame. "Dad, got a minute?"

"Darius. Wasn't expecting you until this evening. Come, sit."

Darius accepted the invitation and rubbed his hands along his thighs as he sat. He hated small talk, one of the things his father suggested he could do to make employees feel comfortable from time to time, but this wasn't the occasion for meaningless chats. He was on a mission to find out what kind of funny business his dad and Andrew had going on while he managed the Texas project.

Darius hunched forward in his seat and rested his elbows on his thighs, his gaze searching his father's for answers to a question he had yet to ask. "I talked to Andrew last week. He mentioned his decision to stay on as CEO."

"*Hmmm*...that." Jeffrey leaned back in his seat, linked his fingers across his belly, and returned Darius' gaze. "I'd like to think we can all come to a reasonable solution that will satisfy everyone involved. For me, that's retirement and being able to step away knowing the two of you can handle the business without damaging everything I've worked for with this power struggle you have going on. But, it looks like you'll have to share CEO responsibilities with Drew if it comes to that."

"How is that fair?"

Did his dad think they were some corporate streaming service like Netflix where he and Drew could both be CEOs? Why would he think that idea to be reasonable? Darius' pride wouldn't allow him to accept that decision. He'd put too much work into McCall Resorts to share what he'd earned with Andrew, someone who hadn't even put in a fourth of the work he had.

Someone who didn't even have an interest in the business, let alone the CEO position until a few months ago.

Darius gritted his teeth, his nose flared, and he fought to control the negative emotions rising within him.

This was his dad's fault.

It was him who wanted Andrew to come home and run the business because he was first born.

It was him who dangled this position like a carrot over Darius' head.

All set to lash out, Darius took a calming breath and relaxed his shoulders. His heart rate slowed, and for the first time in a while, especially when it came to this situation, he considered his words and actions. Blowing up would only prove his father's point that he wasn't ready to lead. Doing so would also reflect that he hadn't learned anything since their last conversation.

"I know this isn't the outcome you wanted, but in business, things change quickly. Sometimes you must compromise. Besides, we're not like any other business. We're a family first, and I expect that you two will come to an agreement by the time we're fully built out in Texas, if in fact, you're ready to lead." The way his father looked over the brim of his reading glasses caused the hairs on the back of Darius' neck to stand.

This conversation was far from over, but he let it go—for now—and stood to leave. "You're right. Family first, so it'll all work out the way it should."

A slow smile spread across his face. He hoped this stunt was one they conjured up to see how he'd react, to see if he'd grown, to test him, because there was no way he planned to share his position with anyone, especially someone who was practically still using training wheels.

# Twelve

After twenty, Kennedy lost count of the rooms Rose McCall led her through. Everything about this house was like something she'd see in a movie or television show—simply unreal.

"Mrs. McCall, I have to tell you that I'm loving this house. If the rest of the resort is half as nice, I'm in for a treat."

Kennedy's favorite rooms so far were the dining room, sunroom, and Jeffrey and Rose's private suite. Rose led her to Nina and Andrew's suite and tapped on the door as she called out to Nina.

"Nina, it's Rose and Kennedy."

Nina flung open the door and threw her arms around Kennedy's neck. "I'm so glad you could make it, although I am quite surprised." Nina released her and raised an inquiring eyebrow. "Is there something you want to tell me?"

Kennedy stole a glance at Rose, who seemed very much interested in an answer from her as well.

"Nope. Nothing at all. Darius invited me, and I accepted—you know for support and honestly, to check this place out. I haven't seen the half of it, and I have to tell you that I'm not disappointed by what I've seen so far."

"*Hmmm.* Okay." Nina folded her arms across her chest. "So how are you supporting Darius today?"

"*Oooh,* you're smooth. I have to watch out for you, even moreso than I thought. We haven't made any plans that I know of. He brought me by here to see you, then I'll be heading to my room to check in."

Nina's eyes near bugged out of their sockets. "What the…? See…that's why he's single. Kennedy, look at all this space. Why aren't you staying here with us?"

Kennedy released a *tsk.* "We're only friends, Nina, so don't read too much into this. Plus, the agreement was for me to come and experience the resort. I have a spa appointment first thing tomorrow morning. I'm dying to check out the Wellness House."

"Well, you won't get any argument from me on that. I didn't want to leave after my first experience."

"And look at her, married with my first grandchild on the way."

"Okay, I see where this is going." Kennedy wagged her finger between Nina and Rose. "Does Darius know y'all are scheming behind his back?" Hadn't he just warned her about his mother less than an hour ago?

"I don't know what you're talking about. I just met you, but I can't speak for Nina. What's the matter with my son anyway? Not attracted to him?"

Kennedy wished she could melt into a puddle and slip down the stairs. Of course, she was attracted to him. Attraction was not their problem.

Kennedy backed away two steps. "Ma'am. Mrs. McCall, Darius is a handsome man, but we don't find it in our best interest to become romantically involved when we work together. It's just not professional."

Nina's grin grew wider. "And so, hopping a plane to come home and meet his family is?"

"You know it isn't like that. We're friends. That's it."

Footsteps pounded up the stairs mimicking her pulse. She jumped when Darius squeezed her arms. She hadn't turned around to confirm it was him, but at this point, she'd grown to know what he smelled and felt like.

"Hey, didn't mean to scare you, friend. Just checking to see if you want to go get settled in your room before dinner."

How much of that had he heard? It wasn't like she lied. They had only established their friendship and nothing more.

"Wait," Nina and Rose called out simultaneously, which even roused Darius' suspicion.

Darius looked between the trio. "What's going on?"

Nina added, "Just wondering if you wanted a home-cooked meal or if you had plans to take Kennedy out to dinner. It'd be nice to have you both stick around for dinner this evening."

"*Ummm,* well, we hadn't made any plans."

Darius rubbed along the side of her arms, burning a hole through her flesh and her heart. She stiffened when she noticed Nina's attentiveness to the interaction and the smile that seemed to grow wider by the second. Poor woman's mouth was about to take over her face.

"Oh, it's fine." Kennedy glanced up at him and then back to Rose and Nina who looked like they were holding their breath. "We're only here for the weekend, so I think it's a good idea to spend time with your family."

"Then it's settled. I'll take Kennedy to her room at the Peach Estate to get her checked in, and we'll come back for dinner."

Darius slid his fingers down her arm until he latched on to her hand and tugged.

"It was nice to meet you, Mrs. McCall, and good seeing you again, Nina. See y'all in a bit."

Darius' timing was perfect. Nina must have convinced Rose that she and Darius were an item or on the road to becoming one, and that couldn't be farther from the truth. Though a nice idea, a relationship between the two of them couldn't work. He'd return home when the project ended. Besides, he was overly consumed with work—business. She didn't fit into his life, and he didn't fit into hers.

∞

Darius escorted Kennedy to the Peach Estate, got her checked in, and showed her to her room. Her fascination with just about everything she'd seen so far brought him a sense of pride. He'd been walking around with his chest puffed out like he built the resort with his hands. And he was attached to the place like that were true, part of the reason it meant so much to him.

After she ogled over her suite, he took her on a brief tour where she experienced the farm-to-table event. The light in her eyes and the sheer joy on her face was everything to him in that moment. And for a second, he entertained the thought of always being the one who had something to do with the joy she experienced.

"I know how much you're looking forward to spending time at the Wellness Center, so I figured I'd take you to look around."

"No."

Darius punched the brakes and snapped his head up to check his rearview mirror. "What's wrong?"

"Sorry. I'm about to get us killed. Don't take me. I want my experience to be fresh tomorrow morning. No preview."

Darius chuckled. "Okay then. We can head on back to the house for dinner if you're ready."

"I am, but are you? How did the conversation go with your dad?"

Darius thought back to their talk, which hadn't done much to ease his anxiety about the situation, and his body became like stone in the driver's seat. He shot a sideways glance at Kennedy, sizing her up to see how much of his feelings he should divulge. At this point, she'd become his confidant and the only person who seemed to understand his feelings about the situation without viewing him as selfish or overly ambitious.

He released a heavy sigh.

"Not as well as I'd hoped." Instead of continuing down the winding path toward the house, Darius pulled over to the side of the road near the farm fields and parked the car. He shifted his weight in the driver's seat so that he faced her. "And I don't think I'll get the answers I want while I'm here either, so I have to apologize for dragging you across the country this weekend because I doubt my problems will be solved in the next day or two."

Kennedy pressed her lips together in a tight line and shook her head. "See, that's where you're wrong. You didn't drag me anywhere. I came willingly because you offered me a free stay at this resort, so I plan to enjoy myself. And you already know what my advice is concerning your family, but

I'm gonna say it again anyway." She covered his hand with hers and squeezed. "Darius, do what you have to do to make your relationship with Andrew right. Becoming CEO can't be the only thing that's important to you. How would you feel if you woke up tomorrow and he didn't? This power struggle will suddenly become meaningless, and you'll regret the fact you didn't mend your relationship when you had the chance."

Darius slipped out of her grasp and rubbed his palms over his face. "I get that. I do. It's just that I've put so much of myself into my work here, and it's like my father doesn't appreciate any of it."

"Did you do it for him or for you?" Kennedy's feather-light voice carried a punch hard enough to trap the air in his chest. Had they been back in Houston, this would have been the precise moment he walked away from her.

How dare she challenge his motivation? How could she—someone he'd only known a few months—see beyond the situation to the root of his problem? A problem he hadn't known he had until now.

"Both." Darius restarted the ignition and pulled back onto the winding road. As fast as the wheels turned, so did his thoughts. It took him thirty-six years to realize that his issue wasn't solely with Andrew, but with his father and the difference in the way he treated the two of them. Darius had worked by his father's side since he was thirteen years old, and all he could recall hearing was how Andrew should have been the one there learning the family business to take over someday.

Why wasn't he enough?

They might not resolve their problems in one weekend, but Darius had no plans to return to Texas without answers.

# Thirteen

Darius latched on to Kennedy's hand like it was the most natural thing in the world—like it was something they made a practice of doing whenever they were together. Besides the fact he simply wanted to enjoy the warm feeling that coursed through him whenever their hands touched, her hand tucked securely in his served as a reminder for him to maintain his cool. She was his special guest, and no matter how the evening ended between him and his brother and father, he'd keep a level head because Kennedy's presence did something to him.

Made him want to be better.

Made him want to be different.

And levelheaded. And all those things his father presented in an earlier speech to him about the type of leader he wanted for McCall Resorts.

"Hopefully, we won't scare you away and make you not want to visit our resort again," Darius bent over and whispered into Kennedy's ear and squeezed her hand before they entered the dining room where Nina and Rose's voices could be heard from the hall.

Kennedy gripped his bicep with her free hand. "Let's hope not, but remember, I'm a friend, and friends don't scare away too easily. I'm here to support you, okay?" She paused, and her dark brown eyes with those shimmering gold flecks bore into his. "Make things right."

For a moment, with the way she looked at him, and the silkiness of her voice flitting over him, he believed he had the power to do just that and much more. Perhaps she had become the strength he always needed. With Kennedy by his side cheering him on and making him believe everything could be alright, it all seemed possible—that is until he escorted her into the dining room and spotted Andrew next to Nina with an I-don't-have-a-care-in-the-world smile. Shouldn't he be as bothered about this situation as him?

Kennedy picked up on his hesitation and gave his fingers a gentle you-can-do-this tug and took the next step forward. Their presence initiated a silence that fell upon the room like a choir quieted by their director. Darius pulled the middle high-back cherrywood chair out for Kennedy and then took the seat to the right of his father.

Rose nodded toward the two of them and flashed a smile that displayed all of her teeth.

*What's going on with her?*

"Glad you two were able to join us. I was starting to think you changed your mind."

Andrew acknowledged Darius with a quick nod. "Yeah. It's good to see you, bro."

Jeffrey piped in, "Welcome, Miss Slaughter."

"Thanks, but please call me Kennedy. Nina, how are you feeling these days? Feeling any kicks yet?"

Nina rubbed her protruding belly and beamed. "Yes…it's the coolest but weirdest feeling. We're still doing pretty good, though I could do without the constant middle-of-the-night-runs to the restroom. Me and this little guy have about four more months together, and then he's getting evicted."

Tickled, the family joined her in laughter.

But then a string of something slithered through him when Andrew bent over and whispered something to her belly. Was it jealousy? Longing? That couldn't be quite right because raising a child hadn't been something he'd put on his long list of things to do, but a quick glance at Kennedy's gushing face told him that it was part of hers.

And that rising silly part of him forcing itself to crush through his common sense wanted to give it to her.

Whatever her heart desired.

Darius downed the glass of water at his place setting hoping the cool liquid would wash those crazy thoughts out of his mind.

Nina asked, "Kennedy, do you want kids?"

Darius choked on the last swallow of water inching down his throat, which did exactly what he didn't want to do—bring attention to himself. "I'm good."

Kennedy shot him a strange look then turned her attention back toward Nina and Andrew. "At some point, yes. I'm a twin, and I couldn't imagine growing up without Kendrick, so I'd like to have two children."

With his squinted eyes, Darius dared Nina to ask him the same question, which he could surmise had already formed in her brain. He'd have to pull her to the side later and assert that she abandon whatever matchmaking scheme she had going on and had apparently roped his mother into. She'd been silent, but from her glossy eyes and the upturned corners of her lips, it was obvious her wheels had been turning. She was practically gushing over future grandchildren that weren't even in the works yet.

She took her cue and brought the conversation back to herself.

"Kennedy, I pray you get exactly what you want one day. But as for me and this little guy, I can't describe how amazing it feels to have life growing inside of me. At one point, I thought I was dying and wouldn't ever get the chance to have a family." She paused and glared between Darius and Kennedy. "That's why I believe it's so important for us to take advantage of the time we have on earth now because we don't know when our time is up. If you want something or someone, I say go after it or him or her."

"Alright, babe. I don't think they're ready for your motivational speeches." Andrew then whispered something in her ear but then apologized as his mother parted her lips. "Sorry. Didn't mean to be rude by whispering."

Rose pushed away from the table and stood. "Please excuse me while I grab dinner."

Kennedy shot up. "I'll come help."

Nina didn't waste a second. "Me, too."

With the women out of the room and out of earshot, Darius and Andrew engaged in a stare down.

"Would you two please stop acting like children?" Jeffrey whisper-shouted through clenched teeth. "I'm about sick of this madness."

Darius recalled his conversation with Kennedy and guarded his words. "You know what, Drew? I don't want there to be any bad blood between us either. You're my brother, and honestly, I should be glad you decided to come home and work with us, but it just feels wrong. I've worked hard for this, and what's messing me up about it is that you don't seem to care and you know it ain't right the way you're handling business."

"Now Darius—" Jeffrey interrupted, but Andrew held up his hand to stop him.

"Let him get it off his chest, Dad. It's obvious he has some stuff going on."

"You're right. I do have some stuff going on. Dad, why is it that I have to work my butt off to prove to you that I deserve to be CEO when all Drew here has to do is show up? He hasn't even worked half as much as I have, yet you have me jumping through hoops to please you."

"That's just it. You won't be ready until you learn that you're not doing this to please me. You're doing it for yourself. What happens when I'm dead and gone? I'll no longer be around for you to please, and then what? Son, everything I have is yours. Yes, you have to work hard, but there's nothing you have to do for me to love you any more or be any prouder of you than I already am. That goes for both of you. The difference between you and Andrew right now is that he chose this because he wants it, not because of me. You're choosing it because you have something you want to prove."

Darius gritted his teeth and took a deep breath. No matter what he said, it didn't seem to get through to his father or Andrew and to continue repeating himself or communicating it with different words was not working to his advantage. What stung the most was that his father said something similar to what Kennedy said earlier, that his motivation was somehow wrong and he was only trying to prove himself worthy to his father. But that couldn't be any farther from the truth. He wanted to run the business because he worked hard for it and he was good at it. Why was any of that even in question?

"This isn't going anywhere. Let's just stick with our current plan to make the decision at the end of the project. By that time, Drew will be a new father, you'll be ready to retire, and it'll be time for us all to move in a different direction. Drew, can you live with that?"

"I'm cool, man. I just want us to be good. Don't want this job coming between us. I'd like for us to work together, figure it out because, look, I'm not trying to come in and step on your toes or take anything away from you. You know that's not my intent."

Women's laughter and steaming trays of meat, vegetables, and dinner rolls cut through the tension, and Darius dropped the subject. He couldn't say he felt better about the situation or that much of anything had been resolved. Deep down, he knew his brother didn't want to intentionally hurt or deceive him, but that job was all he had, all he worked for, and up until now, all he cared about.

While everyone else's attention shifted to the food on the table, commenting on the appearance and aroma, Kennedy's attention rested on him. In a voice as light as a feather that had the ability to melt his heart like that butter drizzling over the dinner rolls on the table, she asked, "You okay? Did y'all talk?"

He nodded. "Yeah, we did."

She studied him as if they were the only two people sitting at the table. "You wanna talk about it later?"

He'd rather not, but if it meant he could spend an extra minute with her, he'd talk about whatever topic she desired to discuss. "Sure. Thanks, sweetheart."

The sentiment slipped from his lips before he could catch it, but seeing the smile it put on her face, he wouldn't dream of taking it back. Kennedy's ears hadn't been the only ones that caught it, though. Nina had practically been engrossed in their business from the beginning, but his mother's head popped up like he'd been speaking to her. Thankfully, she didn't verbally react, but her face spoke for her.

He managed to get through dinner with his family in peace. Work came up once with a discussion of the Texas resort and its progress, but they avoided the pending leadership changes. For the most part of the evening, he observed how Kennedy interacted with his family and their response to her. It was almost as if she were already part of the McCall clan, and he considered that a good thing. Though he hadn't quite settled his issues with his father and brother, that had been the only thing that became more clear tonight—her place in his life.

By his side was exactly where he wanted her to be, but with their work situation, he had to find a way to make that happen.

# Fourteen

The relaxed state that the massage put her in gave her ample time to consider her relationship—or lack thereof—with Darius. Every knead through her back muscles eased the tension in her body but threw her mind into overdrive. She could say that coming to Georgia with him was a bad idea, but the way the massage therapist worked her muscles confirmed that wasn't the truth. The combination of the warm cot, soft meditating music, and peppermint essential oil had been a recipe for love-laced ideas about Darius. No matter how hard she fought to redirect her thoughts during that two-hour massage, Darius dominated them.

Dating him wasn't the worse idea.

They were practically dating now, just without the formal establishment of their whatever-ship. And the way he called her sweetheart last night nearly sent her into a tailspin. Had they been alone, she would've asked him to say it again solely because of how the word sounded to her ears and made both her heart and stomach do somersaults and cartwheels. This should have been a time to refocus and clear her mind of any romantic notions of the two of them, but her heart had grown weary of fighting the feeling.

*Just go with the flow.*

Easy, but hard advice for her. She thrived off having solid, measurable, definite plans.

"Miss Slaughter, your two-hour session has ended, but Mr. McCall left instructions to continue for as long as you need, and afterward you may visit the sauna or quiet room, grab refreshments, and maybe even enjoy a yoga or barre session. If you'd like, you may enjoy a spa manicure and pedicure as well. Your choice, ma'am."

Kennedy's hands trembled from excitement, and her mind raced by the second. So many beautiful choices, and she wanted to experience them all. She'd only been in the Wellness House for a little over two hours, and she'd fallen in love the moment Darius dropped her off that morning.

How on earth had they managed to make her feel like royalty?

The instant she arrived, her host greeted her at the door, and escorted her to a private room to store her things. She undressed, and put on a rob that was softer than silk before being introduced to Sue Ann, her massage therapist.

"Can I just spend forever here?"

Sue Ann chuckled. "I'm sure that can be arranged. How would you like to start your forever?"

A woman could get used to this. "I'll spend a few minutes in the sauna and then on to the reading room."

Sue Ann flashed an accommodating smile. "That's exactly what I would do." She tapped Kennedy's shoulder and winked. "I'll wait for you outside the door. Take your time getting up. No rush."

∞

No phone calls.

No e-mails.

No text messages.

No work.

Nothing or no one to focus on but herself.

Kennedy couldn't remember the last time she'd unplugged, felt good about doing so, and come out on the other side renewed and refreshed. She waited for Darius in the lobby of the Wellness House. A breeze of cool air followed him inside.

"I was starting to think that you'd abandoned me."

"I did—sort of." Kennedy shrugged and grinned. "I think this was the best time I've ever had. Well, I take that back. I know it was the best time I've had. How do people ever willingly leave here? This Wellness House is pure gold. I swear I'm coming back. I could spend an entire week in there."

Darius hiked an eyebrow. "Is that so?"

Kennedy wrapped her arms around his waist and squeezed. "Thank you. If we did nothing else this entire trip, that—" She jammed her thumb toward the double doors that led to pure bliss— "was more than enough."

"If I'm gonna get hugs and smiles from you like that, can I bring you every month?"

"You won't get any protest from me. Promise."

*"Ummm."* Darius settled his eyes on her lips, and he inched forward but restrained himself.

Kennedy cleared her throat to force down the knot that formed from disappointment. His lips against hers would have been the perfect ending to her day at the Wellness House, but they were friends, and kissing would've catapulted them out of the friend zone for sure. But was that the reason he stopped? Or was she giving mixed signals?

Instead, he ran the back of his hands along her cheek and tucked a loose curl behind her ear. Her skin warmed and tingled from his touch all the way down to her toes, something she wouldn't have believed had she not experienced it herself. That whole tingling-and-mouth-drying thing was something that only happened in romance novels and movies, not real life, and certainly not to her. Not in all of her thirty-seven years.

Darius guided her out to his car with his hand resting on the small of her back. It was nice and all, but she kind of wished he'd stop doing that because his gentle touches here and there were starting to drive her crazy.

Crickets, the crisp night air, and the open passenger door of his Beamer greeted her. After he saw her safely inside, he rounded the car and climbed into the driver's seat. "I believe we need to get you something to eat. You've been having *you time* all day, so I guess I should ask if having dinner with me is even something you'd like to do tonight. Would you like to join me for dinner this evening, Miss Kennedy Slaughter?"

"Of course." *I've been alone, but you've occupied my mind all day.*

Darius revved the engine and pulled onto the winding road. At night, the resort was even more beautiful with string lights on every building.

"You'll enjoy dinner at The Barn. To our guests, it's reservation only, but I have a special table and—"

"The Barn? Listen, Darius, I'm all for the experience and all, but I don't think I'm in the mood to eat in a barn."

Darius threw his head back and laughed. "I'm sorry. I should have explained that a little better. It looks a little like a barn, but it's nice—white tablecloths, wine, and fancy food."

Kennedy looked down at her skinny jeans and fitted V-neck shirt. "Oh. Am I dressed okay?"

"You look beautiful. You don't have to change unless you want to. My table is in the back of the restaurant if that helps your decision."

Kennedy assessed Darius' khakis and polo shirt and decided to go with what she was wearing. "Well, in that case, let's go eat some fancy food, but I need fancy good food. I'm hungry."

"Chef Armand is not only an award-winning chef, but he's been with us for so long that he's like family. He rotates between Mick's Chateau and The Barn. He'll take care of you."

"How are you even getting along in Houston with all of this going on back here? This place is amazing. I've only been here a day and a half, and I already don't want to leave."

"Houston isn't that bad, especially now that I have a special friend to hang out with." Darius zipped into the lot and parked in the first available space. He shifted in his seat and caressed her hand. "Thank you for showing that good ol' Texas hospitality, and in case I'm not clear, you're the reason I like being in Texas."

Kennedy clutched her chest with her free hand. "Oh, you're welcome. I wouldn't have it any other way. You turned out to be one of my best clients. After this, you're actually my favorite."

Darius rubbed her chin with his knuckle and tilted it a bit, doing that thing where he acted like he wanted to kiss her but didn't. "I'll do everything I can to stay at the top of your list. C'mon. Let's get some good food."

There it was again. An almost kiss. How'd she get from only wanting to be friends to wanting him to kiss her anyway? When Darius got out of the car, Kennedy took those seven seconds to regroup with a slow, calming breath to clear her thoughts.

*Don't get caught up in the magic of this place.*

Kennedy stepped inside The Barn. One look at the guests screamed she was underdressed. Every woman she saw wore a little black dress or something similar, and she now wished she had changed. But the way Darius' hand rested possessively on her lower back and guided her through the restaurant like she was the Queen of England spoke volumes. She may have been underdressed, but he treated her like they were on a date, and she was in her own little black dress.

Darius pulled her chair from the table and waited for her to sit before taking the seat across from her. Seconds later, a waiter appeared.

"Mr. McCall, how are you this evening? Will you be having the usual peach lemonade?"

"I'm good, Carl. This is my friend, Kennedy. Will you bring a peach lemonade for her to try as well?"

"It's nice to meet you, Miss Kennedy. I'll have those peach lemonades right out for you. Is there anything else I can get for you while you wait?"

"Actually, will you ask Chef Armand to pop over when he gets a moment?"

"Will do."

"Darius, you don't have to bother the chef."

If he was trying to impress her, that wasn't necessary. She'd already been blown away. But one look in his eyes told her different. The man she'd met several months ago may have attempted to throw his weight around, but the man sitting across from her this evening wanted to please her.

Although he hadn't said so, he had a soft spot for her, a revelation that made her melt.

"I know, but he's really good. And besides, I want him to meet you. That way, he'll know to put his special touch on your entrée."

"Say no more. I'm starving, so I need all the special touches on my food tonight."

When Carl arrived with their drinks, Chef Armand appeared next to him, charming Kennedy with a kiss to the back of her hand. She'd looked over the menu but hadn't made up her mind about what to order.

"If you and Mr. McCall don't mind, I'd like to prepare something special for you tonight."

"Chef, you know I'm always open to whatever you prepare, but I'll let Kennedy decide for herself."

"I trust Darius' judgment, but I'm warning you, Chef, I haven't eaten anything of substance all day. I need something good."

"You have my word as long as I can make you something other than salad."

Kennedy chuckled and waved her hand. "Please, anything but that."

"My kinda lady," he said and winked. "Carl will be back with your entrées shortly." Chef Armand whisked away. Carl tucked his notepad in the pocket of his smock and followed.

Darius reached for her hands and held them securely in his grasp, the warmth traveling up her arms sending smoke signals to her brain. She released what she hoped was an unnoticeable calming breath.

"Kennedy, I don't normally mince words, and now isn't the time to start. I think something special is happening between us. Do you agree?"

Kennedy swallowed to moisten her drying mouth. Wasn't this the conversation she wanted to have? In her mind, she'd rehearsed what she would say if the topic of them came up, and she'd even considered bringing it up herself, but now that the subject was on the table, she froze.

His grip loosened a bit, but he didn't let go. "I'm sorry. Have I been reading this all wrong?"

An abrupt "no" escaped her lips, but she softened it. "No, it's just that I wasn't expecting you to say anything about it because of the whole work situation, and you've been introducing me as your friend this whole time. I guess I kinda took that as a hint that you didn't want anything more."

"I want more, Kennedy—with you."

Her heart pounded so loudly she could swear he heard it or at least felt her pulse about to tear through her wrist.

"But what about this project? You don't think going out with me is a conflict of interest?"

"I think we're adults who can manage both. Tell me what you want, Kennedy."

She'd been waiting for him to say those words for the past two weeks, but she didn't expect her heart to be on fire at the sound of them. However, as a woman in charge of her company, she couldn't help but wonder how people would view her for getting involved with a client. Sure, a man would get a pass for doing something like that, but she'd be called unprofessional and probably worse.

Should she follow her heart?

Her heart was what moved her to board the plane with him in the first place.

Her heart was what reminded her of every joyful emotion that arose while she was with him.

And her heart was what connected with his eyes—eyes that saw beyond the president of SCI and into the heart of the woman.

Kennedy slid her hands out of his and reconnected with linked fingers. "I think we owe it to ourselves to give it a shot. The only shots we're sure to miss are the ones we don't take, right?"

Darius lifted her hands to his lips and sent another wave of electricity up her arms when he kissed them. "Right. So, if you're willing, I'd like to officially date you, Kennedy Slaughter."

"I'd like that, too."

The evening evolved into their first official date as a couple with dinner specially prepared by Chef Armand—flank steak with roasted cauliflower and kale for Kennedy and roasted lamb, grilled cauliflower, and carrots for Darius. Chef Armand came out mid-meal to check in on the couple to ensure their satisfaction with their entrees. As far as Kennedy was concerned, this was the best first date she'd ever had.

Great food.

Great company.

In near paradise.

She only hoped following her heart would prove to be the right decision and not counteract with the job she had to do for this man's company. If she ruined either one of them, she ruined both.

# Fifteen

After spending time with Darius' family and enjoying the time spent with him over the last month, Kennedy invited him to have Sunday dinner with her, Mike, and Mabel. She didn't consider herself untidy, but took extra care to ensure her house was presentable. She dusted, purchased a new tablecloth, used her favorite apple-cinnamon plug-in scents, and set the table with some of her best dinnerware.

Kennedy cleaned, seasoned, and injected a small chicken with a garlic butter marinade, and placed it in the oven before she showered and slipped on one of her favorite maxi dresses. The doorbell rang throughout the house. Her heart would've popped out of her chest if that were possible. She checked her watch, noting that it was an hour earlier than their scheduled dinner time.

She took a deep breath and glided toward the door.

*Why am I nervous? I've seen him at least four times over the past week.*

Kennedy tiptoed and peeked through the peephole. Her pulse slowed. She unlocked the door and opened it.

"Well, look at you. Is this why you raced out of church at the end of service?"

Kennedy chuckled and pulled Mabel into her arms for a tight squeeze. "I did not race out of church. I just didn't stick around to chitchat. I wanted to make sure I had everything together for this evening's dinner."

Mabel stepped out of her embrace and walked inside. "*Umm-hmm.* I see." Mabel waltzed toward the kitchen, ran her hand along the new tablecloth, then turned toward Kennedy with a raised eyebrow. "And looks like you've done just that. You must really like him."

"I do," Kennedy admitted. Before now, she'd skated around the topic, but saying it aloud to someone other than Darius freed something within her. She'd been so focused on work that she hadn't allowed herself to do what she wanted. Spending her free time with Darius had been nice.

"It's obvious by the smile on your face and the effort you put in. To be honest, I was starting to think that you didn't own real plates. You usually make us eat off paper plates because you don't want to wash dishes."

Kennedy burst into laughter. "True. True. Well, tonight will be an exception and then we can go back to what you're used to. I don't want to spoil anyone."

Mabel chuckled and waved her off.

Kennedy sat on the couch and patted the seat next to her. When Mabel sat, she asked, "So what do you think about Darius?" Normally, this would be something she'd ask her mom, but since her mom was no longer with her, Mabel had become her fill-in.

"He's ambitious. A bit cocky. But I can see his soft side, especially when it comes to you. That's what's important to me, that he respects you and treats you well. As long as you're happy, then so am I. However, I'm glad he's coming to dinner so that we can learn a little more about the man, Darius, and not the businessman that I'm so used to seeing."

Kennedy patted Mabel's knee. "That's exactly why I invited him. I need a pair of more experienced eyes to help me make sure I'm not rushing or seeing things that aren't there. We've been having such a good time together since we returned from Georgia. Just wanna make sure I'm not living in fantasyland when it comes to this man."

"I doubt that. You always see with your head first, then your heart. I highly doubt you'd be spending the amount of time with him that you are if you had reservations about him."

It wasn't that she had reservations, but she just didn't want to get caught up in him too quickly. But it may already be too late for that. With them spending practically all of their free time together and staying up late on the phone like teenagers, she wasn't sure she wasn't already living and seeing him through rose-colored glasses.

Kennedy stood. "I guess you're right. I'm gonna run and finish my hair before wrapping up dinner. The chicken is in the oven, and the rice is in the rice cooker. I just need to heat the dinner rolls and sauté my zucchini, squash, and carrot medley."

"Need me to do anything?"

Kennedy snapped her fingers. "Oh, yeah. I decided at the last minute to make Arnold Palmers. I have freshly squeezed lemonade and sweet tea chilling in the fridge. Will you go ahead and combine them in the carafe sitting on the counter? I almost forgot."

"Freshly squeezed lemonade? Maybe we need to invite Darius over every time we get together if you're going to treat us like this."

Kennedy chuckled and marched into the master bathroom. She closed the door behind her and gazed at her reflection in the oversized octagon mirror.

Was she overdoing it with the freshly squeezed lemonade?

*Nah, I'm only showing the same kindness I received from his family.*

Kennedy reasoned that she was overthinking the situation and that Darius knew her heart. They were just two people quickly growing fond of each other, enjoying themselves and taking it day by day. The doorbell rang again, and she checked the time. She still had thirty minutes before Darius was scheduled to arrive, so she presumed Mike arrived early and called to Mabel to answer the door. In fifteen minutes, she'd put the finishing touches on her hair and light makeup, which consisted of eye shadow and lip gloss. She walked out of the restroom to greet Mike.

Only, it wasn't Mike.

Darius stood, and she could've sworn her stomach leapt into her throat in sync with his movement from the sofa. "Kennedy, I hope you don't mind me coming earlier than planned. I tried calling, but got your voicemail."

Her phone must still be set to silent from church service that morning. She moved closer and embraced him. "It's not a problem at all. I think I have everything covered, but I appreciate you volunteering."

"Are you just saying that because you think I'll ruin dinner?"

Kennedy snickered. "Of course not. Everything is about done, except veggies. I can handle that. If you want, you can come to the kitchen and keep me company." She moved toward the kitchen, but paused and directed her attention to Mabel. "Aunt Mabel, have you heard from Mike?"

"He just called. Said he tried to reach you, too. Wanted to know if he needed to stop by the store to bring anything. He should be here in the next ten minutes or so."

Kennedy led Darius to the kitchen. She stopped and gasped when she caught sight of a bouquet of red and white roses placed on the table in front of her place setting. She turned to Darius, who sported a smile that nearly melted her heart like butter in a hot pan.

"Those are for you. Your aunt Mabel suggested I leave them there to surprise you."

Kennedy peered around him and caught a glimpse of Mabel. She winked and waved a box of chocolates in the air.

"Thank you. These are beautiful." Kennedy sauntered toward the crystal vase and sniffed the bouquet.

Darius closed the distance between them and took one of her hands in his, setting it on fire. "Just like you."

Kennedy wrapped her arms around his waist and squeezed. His cologne was different today. More rustic and earthy. Maybe he wanted to impress her just as much as she wanted to impress him. She pulled her bottom lip between her teeth and smiled. They were on the same page.

Kennedy broke the embrace first and cleared her throat. She could have easily stood wrapped in his arms another fifteen minutes, but her grumbling stomach won the battle. "Okay, just a couple more minutes, and I'll have the veggies ready."

Kennedy removed the chicken from the oven to cool and placed a sheet pan of dinner rolls in the oven. She maneuvered around the kitchen to gather the pre-cut vegetables, seasoning, oil, and skillet. While she finished up dinner, Mike arrived and joined the two of them in the kitchen, along with Mabel. They engaged in small talk until dinner was set on the table.

Kennedy removed the flowers and placed them near the kitchen window to absorb the sunlight.

After they'd washed their hands and taken their seats—Kennedy and Darius sat across from Mabel and Mike—Mabel blessed the food.

Mike started the conversation after his first bite of baked chicken. "So Darius, what are your intentions with Kennedy? She's like a sister to me, and I don't want to see her hurt. She's been through enough."

Darius swallowed the food in his mouth and wiped his lips with the napkin. He glanced at Kennedy, then back at Mike. "I enjoy Kennedy's company. We're just getting to know each other right now. I've been clear about my intentions with her. I don't have anything to hide, and I'm not seeing anyone else. I'd like to think we can build upon what we've already started and see where this thing between us leads."

Mike continued. "So, what happens when the resort is finished? You just return to Atlanta? What happens then?"

That had been a concern of Kennedy's, but she and Darius hadn't discussed it yet, though she believed it was something they could handle when the time came.

"I'd like to think we could work something out. Me staying in Houston is not out of the question."

Kennedy's heart raced at the possibility. The tremors sent signals to her hands, and she dropped her fork.

"Excuse me." Kennedy stood and placed that fork in the sink and returned with a clean one.

"Kennedy, I like that you're happy, but I just want to make sure your eyes are open. You guys know that long-distance relationships rarely work. I know it's early in your relationship, but if you think you might have a future together, think about this kind of stuff now."

"Thanks, Mike. I think we're okay at the moment." Kennedy shot Mabel a save-me look. Wasn't that the reason she asked them all over? So that they could help her see this thing with Darius from a different perspective? "I appreciate you looking out for me. You've always been like a brother to me, so I don't take your advice lightly, but I think Darius and I will be able to handle it if it comes to that."

But what if it did come to that and Darius decided he wouldn't stay in Houston? She couldn't move to Georgia, not when she had her brother's company to run.

Perhaps this was a conversation she and Darius needed to have sooner rather than later.

# Sixteen

Darius wished there was some way he could reassure Kennedy about their future, but he didn't know what it held for them. Kennedy said they could handle it if their relationship progressed and one of them would have to move, but he didn't believe her. He wasn't entirely sure she believed it either. He noticed that she blinked rapidly when she was uncertain about something, and her eyelids had fluttered like butterfly wings a few moments ago.

All he knew was he had no intentions of hurting her or to stop seeing her. He'd never enjoyed another woman's company as much as he enjoyed hers. He'd do whatever it took to keep that going, even if that meant flying to Houston every weekend to see her.

Mabel piped in. "Mike, settle down. These are two smart, grown folks. They can handle themselves. I'm sure they knew what they were getting into when they started dating."

"Thanks, Miss Mabel. Mike, you don't have to worry. Kennedy's well-being is important to me, too."

He'd almost said that her heart was safe with him, that her happiness was at the forefront of his mind, but he shook those sentiments off. Though his feelings were growing for her in ways he'd yet to experience before now, his large bite into his dinner roll and caution stopped his lips from speaking any further.

In a sense, those sentiments sounded more like his brother, Andrew, and not him. He could not morph into the lovesick puppy that Andrew had become for Nina.

"That's all I need to know." Mike took a bite of his food and chewed before he continued. He pointed his fork in Darius' direction. "You know I'm gonna hold you to that, right? Don't let me down, bro."

Darius acknowledged Mike with a fist bump.

For now, Mike seemed satisfied with his responses. Mabel took over the conversation with more questions about his family and their business.

"You know, Darius, I'm excited for the opening of your family's Houston resort. What's next for you after this? Any plans to open resorts in other cities?"

"No plans as of yet. My job is to ensure the success of this new resort so that'll be my primary focus for a while."

That, and working on becoming CEO. "Because this is my project, I foresee myself spending a lot of time in Houston, even after its completion, so Kennedy will have a tough time getting rid of me."

Both Mabel and Kennedy chuckled. Mike smirked but continued to eat his food. He'd fallen into the big brother role well. Darius could sense Mike was still sizing him up, which was different behavior for him. In their interactions involving the project, Mike had been professional, kind, and easygoing. Darius surmised the dynamics of their relationship had changed when he started dating Kennedy. He couldn't blame Mike though. He'd probably behave the same way if he had a sister, no matter her age.

Kennedy took a bite of her vegetables, chewed, and swallowed. Her lingering gaze lit a fire in his heart. "I have no desire to get rid of you."

The smile that teased the corners of her lips tugged on his heart strings. There went those emotions bubbling within him again.

Darius rubbed his chest and returned the smile. "That's good to know."

"We're still sitting here," Mabel blurted.

Kennedy and Darius laughed.

An audience was the only thing that prevented him from covering her lips with his.

Darius continued to talk with Mabel and Kennedy throughout dinner from discussions about where he went to school and what life was like growing up on a resort to lighter topics like what he enjoyed about the Houston area during his time there. Mike seemed to lighten up as time went on and joined in the conversation. He shared a couple of stories about him, Kennedy, and her late twin brother, Kendrick, growing up.

After dinner, the group enjoyed slices of turtle cheesecake. Mabel and Mike left shortly after dessert. Darius stayed behind to help Kennedy clean up the kitchen.

Darius placed the last dish in the dishwasher and pressed the start button. "Dinner was really good. I appreciate the invitation."

Kennedy finished wiping down the countertops and stepped into his arms. "You're welcome. Figured it's the least I can do after the great time you showed me in Georgia. I hope Mike wasn't too hard on you."

Darius leaned against the counter but didn't release his hold around her waist. "Nah. I understand him. I think I would've done the same thing if I had a sister. You're a kindhearted, beautiful woman. He's just looking out for you."

"Yeah, he's been like that my whole life. He's pretty much a brother to me, but he's been hurt before, so I think he's just making sure that it doesn't happen to me, if he can help it."

Darius placed a gentle kiss against her forehead. His lips warmed from the touch. Fire burned within his chest.

"I care about you, Kennedy, so I promise to do my best not to hurt you. You have my word."

Darius' heart drummed. Those foreign feelings returned.

Feelings he didn't know what to do with.

He had to get out of there before he made a fool of himself. He didn't know how to manage whatever emotions were coursing through his heart and mind.

"It's getting late so it's about time for me to leave and for you to rest. I'll call you when I make it home and get comfortable."

"Sounds good."

Kennedy walked him to the door. He gave her one final hug before he strode to his car and climbed behind the wheel. Darius waved before he backed out of her driveway. He'd hoped the strong percussion rhythm of his heart would slow down once he left her, but it continued during the thirty-minute drive back to his apartment.

What did these feelings even mean and what was he supposed to do about them? That left him with two hurdles to cross: figuring out his next move at McCall Resorts and figuring out how to deal with his emotions as they related to the beautiful Kennedy Slaughter.

∞

Life was going her way.

For the first time since her brother's death a little over a year ago, Kennedy's smile was genuine. SCI's projects were all moving according to plan. Her relationship with Darius strengthened with each passing day.

Kennedy waltzed into the office, forcing herself to focus on the work that lie ahead. Her evening date with Darius consumed her thoughts. She mentally searched through her closet for the perfect dress to wear to tonight's dinner.

On autopilot, she went through her normal routine. Booting up her computer, brewing her morning coffee, and walking through the office to speak to employees who were already at their desks.

She returned to her desk, took her first sip of coffee, and clicked through e-mails. She read the first three lines of a message with the subject, Contractor Delay, and the coffee she'd just drank made her sick to the stomach. It didn't bring about that normal feeling of relaxation and readiness to take-on-the-world jolt that it normally gave her.

Mike tapped on the door and simultaneously entered.

"We need to talk about the effect the recent rainstorm has had on the McCall Resort project."

*Please don't let this be problem number two.*

Mike sat in a visitor's leather seat across from her desk, hunched forward, and rested his elbows on his knees.

"While we budgeted for weather-related delays, we didn't account for the recent and projected storms. Because the ground is saturated and we're expecting heavy storms off and on for the next two-and-a-half weeks, it's not feasible for the construction vehicles to begin the dig for phase three of the project. I don't want you to worry, but wanted to keep you informed. Our primary goal during this time is to prevent cave-ins. The site has already been prepared against such circumstances, so we're on top of that."

"Okay. Is there anything else we can do while this passes?"

"Well, you know how the weather is here. If the storms miss our area, then the grounds will dry up faster and we can get back to work. We've made significant progress already, with some parts of the project already ahead of schedule. I wouldn't worry much, but it's a conversation we need to have with the client."

Kennedy nodded and massaged her temples. "Right. While I have you here, we need to talk about Greg's project. Apparently, his crew is down with a virus, so they won't be able to start next week as planned. You're copied on the e-mail. Have you read it yet?"

Mike whipped out his phone, opened up his messages, and read the e-mail. Mike reassured her. "We'll have this discussion with the client. The ground is saturated, so we can't start next week anyway."

Kennedy heaved several deep breaths.

"We'll be okay, Kennedy. You don't have to start worrying until I worry. And does this look like the face of a man who's worried?" Mike pointed to his relaxed features. "But I know this side of things is different for you and you're a stickler for schedules. Everyone involved in these projects knows there will be setbacks. Just let me handle it. It's all good." Mike stood and marched toward the door. He turned and called over his shoulder before he left. "Loverboy will understand."

Darius would likely understand, but she didn't like it one bit. She'd been spending too much time with him to the point where she wasn't focused on what was happening around her. She needed to be more involved in her own business. At this rate, it seemed Mike was doing her job and his. As much as she enjoyed her time with Darius, she had to pull back.

Kennedy sent him a text to cancel tonight's date.

Operation Get Her Head Back in the Game was now in full effect.

# Seventeen

Darius' standing weekly project update meeting was less than an hour away, followed by lunch. He stared back at his reflection while he groomed himself. He'd been so busy with work over the past week that he hadn't spent any time with Kennedy. Their conversations had been reduced to text messages. Dry text messages. Life seemed empty without any real contact from her. Something was missing.

Kennedy was missing.

When he arrived in SCI's parking lot, he wasted no time climbing out of his car to get inside.

"Good morning, Mr. McCall. You're about fifteen minutes early today. Can I get you coffee or doughnuts?"

"I'm fine. Thanks, Miss Mabel. Is Kennedy in the conference room?"

"Not yet. She's in a meeting with Mike. Give her another few minutes, and she'll be ready for you. Are you sure there's nothing I can get for you?"

"I'll take that coffee, but I can grab it myself."

"Come on back." Mabel escorted him to the breakroom and hung in the doorway while he prepared his coffee. Her eyes burned a hole through his back, and he turned and flashed a smile.

"I gotta tell you that I'm looking forward to spending a little time at the resort when you all are up and running here."

"You've been so good to me these past few months, I'll see about getting you a free stay. How does that sound?"

"I'd say it sounds like you're trying to win my heart, but we both know it's not my heart you're after." She smiled and winked.

Before he could protest, she added, "But I'll take you up on that free stay. I want to know what it's like to be treated like a queen, too."

Was that the term Kennedy used to describe her time at the resort? As far as he was concerned, she deserved that and more any and every day.

"You have my word." Darius stirred in cream and sugar and secured the lid on his cup.

He followed Mabel to the conference room, and his ears perked up at the sound of voices, one of which clearly belonged to Kennedy. When he stepped into the room and locked eyes with her, his heart sank. The bright, welcoming eyes he'd come to know didn't shine as bright and held a hint of sadness. Her smile was missing. Her face was stoic and expressionless, much like the time they first met when he insulted her.

"Mr. McCall, glad you're here. We're ready to get started."

Mike sat to her right, and his expression wasn't any better than hers. And Darius didn't miss the fact she referred to him as Mr. McCall. Not only had they established months ago that she should call him Darius, but their budding relationship was far beyond formalities.

Something was wrong.

He walked as if treading thin ice on the way to his seat across from Mike.

∞

Someone may as well have taken her heart and squeezed it between their fingers like a piece of Play-Doh.

At least that's the way it felt when disappointment laced Darius' face when she referred to him as Mr. McCall—a formality that they'd long since passed. But that was her way of setting the tone for the meeting and keeping the lines straight. He may even request she no longer call him Darius by the time the meeting ended.

"Good morning, Kennedy, Mike." He nodded toward Mike but kept his eyes on her. *Ugh.* That's what she got for mixing business and pleasure.

"Okay, so we'll jump right in. Let me be the first to apologize, Mr. McCall, but we've encountered a delay in your project, one we couldn't foresee, but please accept our apologies and know that we're doing everything we can to get the project back on track. Our drywall contractor is currently facing labor issues. Their laborers are on a strike over their pay. The laborers haven't shown up in the past three days, and the truth is we're not sure how long this will last, but in the meantime, we're reaching out to some of our backup contractors. I have to manage your expectations though because many of them don't have the capacity for this work, and with the issues due to the recent storms, this could set us back at least a month if our current contractor doesn't rectify his laborer situation."

There.

She'd delivered the bad news.

The news that kept her awake for the past couple of nights.

The news that solidified her choice to put the brakes on their relationship.

Was there something she could have done to intervene and jump ahead of the situation?

If she couldn't fix this fast, who knew what this would do to SCI's reputation? And how would this affect them securing future jobs?

Kennedy held her breath and waited for Darius to process the bomb she'd dropped. She knew how important this job was to him, and she hated to be the one to interfere with his goals because this project not going right not only affected her, but him as well. His face contorted, and his eyebrows hiked up and down several times as he took in the information. His disappointment was evident, but his response surprised her.

"I understand. I'll update my team this afternoon. Have you figured out how this will affect the budget?"

Mike jumped in after words eluded Kennedy. She'd braced herself for a fight for the past two days, certain that Darius would lose his mind and somehow pin the blame on her. Who was he, and what had he done to the man she'd met a few months ago? Still, she held her breath, waiting for the moment when he'd lose it.

She watched as he and Mike discussed the project like professionals. It seemed she was the one who had lost all professionalism. Mike explained how they could move the timeline up for other parts of the project while the labor issue got sorted out to minimize the loss of time—a solution that would also have the least impact to the budget. Relief washed over her because of Mike at her side. His expertise and management proved once again that she sat in the wrong chair.

An hour later, after Mike led Darius through their strategy, softening the blow of the delay, Darius' features relaxed. "Thanks for your hard work, brother."

"That's what we're here for. SCI takes pride in keeping our clients happy and being with you through post construction." Mike stood. "That's all I have for today. I'm gonna head on out to the site. Kennedy, call me if you need me."

Kennedy nodded, impressed Mike held a level of calm she didn't seem to possess. She'd been freaking out for the past few days, although he assured her they could get through it and would likely still complete the project on time. *Delays are budgeted into the timeline*, he reminded her. Still, it didn't make her feel any better, especially when so much was riding on this project's completion.

"Kennedy, we need to talk," Darius said after Mike left the room.

"Sure. Is there any additional info you need that Mike didn't provide?"

Darius slid his chair about six inches closer to hers and rested his weight on the conference table. "I'm not talking about the project, and I think you know that, but I don't want to talk here. Are we still on for lunch?"

Kennedy managed to mask her anxiety through the meeting and sucked in a breath to keep her voice even and calm. "With everything happening, do you think that's a good idea? I mean, this project has hit a pothole, and I need to keep my head."

Darius covered her trembling fingers and squeezed. "Kennedy, you do realize that there's nothing you could have done to prevent this issue. It's just one of those things beyond our control. And like Mike said, we do what we can to work around it. I'm not trippin' about it, so why are you?"

"Because, Darius, if word gets out that SCI screwed up this project, what do you think will happen to our reputation? This is the biggest project we've ever had. Don't you think potential clients will laugh us out of the room if we can't handle this? No one will take us seriously. You have to understand that I have to get this right."

"It sounds like you need a listening ear. How about a quick lunch—somewhere nearby where you can be close enough if someone needs you? A few minutes away from the office will do you some good."

"Okay. Thirty minutes."

"I'll take it."

Kennedy went to grab her things while Darius waited for her at the elevator bank. On her way past Mabel, who she had no intention of stopping to chat with, she called out to her, "Kennedy, no need to rush back after lunch. We'll call you if we need you."

Kennedy planted a hand on her hip and cocked her head to one side. If she didn't know any better, she'd think Darius and Mabel had somehow gotten together to conspire against her. In a hushed tone, Kennedy hissed, "You know things are too crazy around here for me to take long lunches."

"And what you keep forgetting is that you are the boss of a competent team. Everything is under control. I promise to call you if we need you. Take your time. He's a special client."

That wink Mabel tagged on warned Kennedy that she'd put on her matchmaking auntie hat, so Kennedy backed off because she knew when she'd lost. She could deal with her aunt anytime, but for now, she had to come up with

a way to let Darius down easy—at least take a break until

they finished his project.

# Eighteen

Despite his efforts to convince Kennedy otherwise, Darius agreed with her request to put space in between them until the project was completed. And the only reason he agreed was because he thought she'd change her mind after they returned to their routine of weekly meetings followed by lunch. But each week, she finagled her way out of lunch or insisted on a teleconference if there were no major updates. And spending time with her on weekends was out of the question because there was always something work-related that required her attention.

She'd managed to lock him out emotionally and it frustrated him. How could she switch her feelings on and off?

He played her game long enough, and it was high time she stopped fighting the connection they shared so they could get on with their life together. Darius rubbed his hands over his face and blinked several times.

When had he become an emotional wreck? Or even allow his emotions to have a voice? It had to have something to do with the fact that he was on a flight back to Georgia to meet his nephew. Though he still had unresolved issues with his brother and father, he wouldn't miss the birth of his nephew—the baby hadn't done anything to him—and he wasn't in the business of punishing children for the parents' errors.

If he hadn't learned anything else from being with Kennedy, she taught him to cherish family. Aside from his work, family was all he had. And although he'd prefer to go a few rounds in a boxing ring with Andrew right now, he could press pause to congratulate him on this new journey into fatherhood.

A fleeting thought surfaced in his mind about the time when he'd be able to take that journey into fatherhood, but he dismissed it. When had children become something he desired to have?

The plane's gyration from touching down on Hartsfield Jackson International Airport's runway jolted him from his thoughts, a welcomed distraction from his emotions bouncing all over the place. He only brought carry-on luggage, so when he deplaned, he strode to the passenger pickup area where his father waited for him. Darius tossed his luggage into the open trunk before climbing into the passenger seat.

"Hey, son. How was your flight?"

"Not bad. Have I missed Baby Drew's grand entrance?"

"Nah. Nina is still in labor, and poor Andrew is about to lose his mind."

Darius chuckled. "I'm sure he'll be alright."

Jeffrey merged the luxury car into the traffic circle and exited the airport. He cleared his throat. "How's Kennedy? We all thought she'd be traveling with you."

"Work has her tied up." That was mostly true. And frankly, he didn't invite her on this trip, though she would have come to see the baby. Call him selfish, but if she were flying to Atlanta with him, he wanted it to be because she wanted him and their relationship, not solely to check in on

Nina and the baby. He'd like to believe that what they had was more meaningful than her friendship with Nina.

"I see." A few beats of silence passed before Jeffrey added, "Anything you need to get off your chest? We have about forty minutes before we get to the hospital."

Darius and his father had never discussed his relationships before, but until this point, he hadn't met anyone worth discussing with his father. And given the fact he and his father had their own issues to iron out, Darius couldn't decide if talking about Kennedy would make any difference, so he fixed his gaze out of the passenger's side window. "Nah, Dad. I'm good."

"Well, you look like you done lost your puppy." Jeffrey shot a sideways glance at Darius. "Women can be hard to figure out, so if you ever need any help trying, I'm here. Not saying I have all the answers," he said, chuckling. "In fact, I don't have any, but I'm here to listen."

Darius lounged his head back against the fine leather seat. "I wish I knew what to say, but I don't. I mean, I get it. I understand that she has to focus on SCI, but she has to have a life outside of work. When we're done building the resort, then she'll reconsider our relationship. But what happens when there are issues on the next project? Will she back away then, too?"

"*Hmmm*. She sounds a lot like you. For the past two years, your mother and I have tried to encourage you to get a life outside of McCall Resorts. Ambition is good, but you can't spend your life with titles, nor can you go on dates, eat dinner with them, or lie with them at night."

"I'm finally starting to get it now, but what will it take for her to get it?"

"I wish I had a better answer for you, but it's one of those things she'll have to come to terms with on her own. I don't know if there's anything you can do or say to convince her otherwise. If it's meant to be, you two will find your way back to each other."

"That sounds like something Mom would say."

"After forty years of marriage and the influence of her Hallmark movies, what can I say?" He chuckled. "But I believe it to be true, and so does your mother."

"What do you mean?"

"Let's just say that she and Nina are heavily invested in you two. They probably want to see y'all together more than you want it."

"Mom just has her mind on more grandkids. I'm not sure what Nina's motivation is."

"There's that, but I speak for your mother and me when I say we want you to be happy. We can rest easy knowing you found more to life than work."

Darius gaped at his father like he'd grown another head. "Wow. She really has gotten to you, hasn't she?"

"Consider this your heads-up. The one thing that'll save your hide this time is all attention is on the entrance of Junior."

"He deserves the spotlight anyway. I can handle Kennedy."

Jeffrey snorted, but didn't comment further on the Darius-Kennedy situation.

Darius resisted the urge to whip out his phone to text her during the remainder of their drive to the hospital. There was no other way to describe how he felt, but helpless. That hollow feeling that had taken up residence in his heart and belly was unwelcome, yet the only way he knew and wanted to fill that space was with Kennedy. At least while he was away, the arrival of his nephew would keep his mind off the fact that he'd finally encountered a situation that his degrees and business expertise couldn't help him solve.

∞

Disinfectant assaulted his senses.

Darius and his father sat in the hospital waiting room, accompanied by Nina's assistant, Danielle, and his uncle Thaddeus. They'd only been inside twenty minutes, and with the temperature set to freezing during the month of September, his thoughts drifted to Kennedy and how heat emanated from him whenever she was around.

What had she done to him? And who had he become?

Darius hunched forward in his seat and ran his hand along the back of his neck. *I can't even identify what I'm feeling and why this situation is making me so crazy.*

Their phones pinged simultaneously. Darius checked the notification, thankful for the distraction, to see pictures of Andrew McCall, Jr.

"Dad, he looks just like Drew. Congrats. You're a pawpaw now."

Danielle gushed and Thaddeus added his congratulatory remarks.

A slither of discomfort rolled around his belly at the sight of his father's eyes misting. He'd been right: Babies change people. Other jumbled emotions crashed through him, too.

Emotions better left unidentified.

He forwarded the pictures to Kennedy who responded with a phone call. "Darius, I thought the plan was for us to go to Atlanta together when Nina had the baby."

Darius stood and walked away from the group before he responded. "Yeah, but that was before you pumped the brakes. I just figured you'd changed your mind about this trip, too."

"Darius, that's not fair. You're punishing me for my choices."

"I don't think you're the one who's being punished here, Kennedy. For the last few weeks, all I've done is try to reconnect with you, but you keep pushing me away. How was I supposed to know this would be an exception?"

Darius heard her exaggerated sigh through the line, which in turn, frustrated him. The silence that followed engulfed him like Jonah in the belly of the whale.

"Okay. Let's try this again. How are Nina and the baby?"

"Fine as far as I know. We haven't seen them yet. Dad; Nina's assistant, Danielle; Uncle Thad; and me are all here in the waiting room. Mom and Drew are in the delivery room with her."

"She's well cared for then, I'm sure. Will you give her my love and let her know I'll be out to see her as soon as I can?"

"Anything for you."

"Thank you. I'll be in touch. Enjoy your family."

Kennedy ended the call like there was nothing more for the two of them to discuss, when in his mind, the most important topic had been left untouched. Shouldn't pressing pause on their relationship also mean she'd do the same when it came to her connection to his family?

The one thing he should be focused on right now was where his role in the company was headed now that Drew had become a father and their Houston area resort was near completion, but even that couldn't hold his focus when Kennedy held his heart hostage.

He turned to find his mother standing in the doorway of the waiting room with a smirk planted on her face. "Anything for you? I take it that was Kennedy?"

He ignored her comment and advanced into her arms for a quick embrace. "Congratulations, Grandma."

"Oh, Li'l Drew is the most precious thing. I can't believe one of my babies has had a baby."

"Mom, Drew is a grown man. Dude is far from a baby."

"As far as I'm concerned, both of you will always be my babies, so I'm putting you on notice, mista. Get your act together because I'd like to see you both happy with families of your own one day."

He refused to have the Kennedy conversation again. "I hear ya, Mom." He planted a soft peck on her cheek and returned to his seat. "When can we go see them?"

"Once they're all cleaned up and transferred to their room. Your brother is really happy that you're here, Darius."

With this rift they'd been carrying on because of their roles in McCall Resorts, Darius couldn't quite blame Andrew if he thought he wouldn't show up, but Andrew had to know that he wouldn't miss such a special occasion. He'd put his beef on hold to welcome his nephew into the world. Besides, his issue wasn't with Junior, it was with his father.

"Drew knows I wouldn't miss it."

Before Rose could part her lips to continue with a conversation he'd rather not have, he jumped back in. "I know you've got more pics of the baby. Let's see 'em."

Distraction successful.

She gave play-by-play details of the delivery until Andrew called her with the room number.

Darius entered Nina's room last—after Danielle, who rushed to her side and kissed her forehead. Signage with a blue blanket bundled around a stork's beak covered the door with the McCall name written on it. Andrew coddling the baby next to Nina's bedside drew his attention first. Certain he'd never seen his brother as happy as he was in that moment, Darius was almost jealous. A similar joyful-like expression laced his face when he talked about or was with Nina, but right now was a new level.

"Congrats, bro. Congrats, Nina. How're you feeling?"

"Like someone released the air out of a balloon, a little pain, but it was all worth it to meet this little guy." Nina leaned forward and stretched her neck, attempting to get a glimpse past Darius. He also turned in that direction. "Where's Kennedy? Last we talked, she said she'd come."

"She asked that I give you her best and to let you know she'll be out here as soon as she can."

Nina darted her eyes toward Rose, and they communicated without speaking before Nina shook her head like she was disappointed. Not in the fact that Kennedy wasn't there, but in him. How did this become his fault?

"Okay," Nina said slowly. "I'll give her a call later."

"D, would you like to hold him?"

Darius strode to Andrew's side and crouched down next to the rocking chair. "I think I'll let you enjoy this moment. I'll get my chance later. I'm proud of you, bro. You did good."

"That means a lot coming from you." Andrew lowered his voice to where only Darius could hear. "You know I've kinda set the bar high so they'll be wondering when you're gonna settle down."

"They might just have to wait a while longer."

"Whatever you plan to do, you need to work fast. I'm rethinking this CEO thing. I want to make sure I'm around for this little guy."

Hadn't those been the exact words he'd expected and craved to hear from Andrew? Yet, the rush and the power he thought he'd feel didn't come. From the beginning, he'd counted on Andrew choosing his family over his position at

McCall Resorts, but the thought of him being CEO instead of Andrew without this thing worked out with Kennedy only accelerated the anxiety that coursed through him. It was time for an addendum to his original plan.

# <u>Nineteen</u>

Lauren Dorsey.

Boutique owner with the style and physique of a supermodel. Beautiful. Successful. Prominent family.

Darius invited Lauren out to dinner at Morton's The Steakhouse in Downtown Atlanta. It was the most he could do to take his mind off Kennedy. He and Lauren had gone out a few times in the past, but their relationship never developed into anything. He found her attractive, but he never sensed that connection with her like he shared with Kennedy. From the moment he met Kennedy and shook her hand, he knew something was special about her.

But with Lauren, things were different. And now that he'd been down that emotional road with Kennedy, perhaps he could open himself up with Lauren since they had a bit of history. Maybe. They spent most of dinner with small talk. Safe topics. Holidays. Atlanta Braves. Family.

"I've heard good things about your family's business expanding into Texas. I'm really proud of you. You talked about that a couple of years ago—set a goal and went for it. I've always liked that about you."

Lauren reached across the table and covered his hand with hers.

Nothing.

That's what he felt.

She may as well have been a stranger.

"Thanks, Lauren. We have about three months left until our Houston resort is complete. Maybe you should visit sometime." That was the polite thing to say. Wasn't it? He didn't care if she ever visited. All he could think about was Kennedy and what she might be doing right now. Was she missing him as much as he missed her?

"I might do that. How are your mom and dad? And I see Andrew's back with a wife." She took a bite of her chocolate cake.

"Everybody's good. Andrew's wife, Nina, just gave birth to a little boy."

Lauren gushed and drew her hands to her chest. Her eyes held that longing that he'd recognized within himself earlier.

He needed to get out of there before Lauren got some crazy idea that he wanted that kind of life with her.

He didn't.

"Please give Andrew my well wishes."

"I will. In fact, I should be getting back to the hospital to check in on them."

Darius and Lauren talked more about her boutique while he waited for the check and paid for their dinner. As she talked, he remembered one of the reasons he wasn't that into her. She was too into herself. Come to think of it, they talked about her most of the night. He didn't mind as much because it kept his mind off his issues with Kennedy. At least for a little while.

He walked her to her car, then climbed into his own, but didn't start the ignition. He sat with his elbow resting against the door. Thoughts of Kennedy ran rampant through his mind.

*Woman, what have you done to me and how are we gonna work this out?*

∞

If Darius thought going to Atlanta without her would get her to change her mind about their relationship, he thought wrong.

He had plenty of opportunity to bring up the fact that he planned to travel home. As much as he broached the subject of their relationship—or lack thereof—he could have asked if she still planned to attend. Kennedy fumed, incessantly tapping her pen on the wooden desk.

*Technically, I shouldn't be upset.*

She was the one who suggested they put a temporary hold on their relationship until SCI finished the project.

Maybe traveling with him would have sent the wrong message. She couldn't be certain if she was upset because he left without her given how much he proclaimed to care or if her displeasure stemmed from not being there for Nina like she promised. Over the past several months, they'd grown quite close, but if she were to be honest with herself, she wanted Darius to care more and push for her to come along with him, even if the answer was no. Yeah, she was wacko.

Two taps on the door signaled her aunt Mabel's entrance. No one tapped that way but her. "Come in." Thank goodness for the distraction.

"Just checkin' in to see if you'd like me to bring you something back for lunch."

"I'm okay. I may place an order for delivery when I get hungry."

"Alright, if you say so." Mabel all but chanted her displeasure and posted her frame against the doorjamb.

"Is there something else I can help you with?"

"Well, since you asked." Mabel closed the door behind her and claimed the visitor's seat across from Kennedy's desk. "It's time that I give you my unsolicited opinion, and since it's officially the lunch hour, I'm giving myself permission to speak about your personal life during business hours."

"Aunt Mabel, can we do this la—"

Mabel thrust her palm up and stopped Kennedy in her tracks. "There's no one else around to tell you when you're going overboard, so I've appointed myself. Kennedy, you're like a daughter to me, and I understand the dilemma you have with trying to do right by this company and honor your brother's memory, but you can't allow your commitment to the dead to overshadow your commitment to the living."

Kennedy gasped.

"Now hear me out. I'm talking about you, sweetheart. I know you love your brother—we all do—but you're still here, and you need to live the life you have. My God, you only get one of them. I've told you time and again over the past months that you're a great leader, and this company is thriving under your leadership. So, what's the real reason you stopped seeing Darius before you even gave the relationship a solid chance?"

Kennedy opened her lips, but no words came.

"Honey, close your mouth if you don't plan to speak. Ya gonna let flies in."

Kennedy snorted and doubled over in laughter, but still didn't answer Mabel's question. Mabel reached across the desk and took Kennedy's hands in hers.

"When you were born, I made a promise to your mother that I'd always look after you. Now, tell me how I can help. What's really going on between you and Darius? We're all rooting for you."

"We?"

"Don't give me that look. Nina has been conspiring for the longest time. How do you think I got the idea to play sick? So that you would ask Darius to go painting with you in my place?"

Kennedy yanked her hands away and clapped. "I knew it. I knew something was up. I just couldn't put my finger on it. I can't believe y'all."

"Well, sometimes people need a little nudging, and it's clear the two of you are a little slow in this department, so again, what's the problem?"

Kennedy sat back in her cushioned seat, and her expression turned serious. "Auntie, you know how important it is to me to present the right image—you know, be seen as a competent professional. Even Darius had his doubts about me in the beginning. I don't want to give anyone else another reason to doubt me. If I'm going to do this job, I want to do it right and give my best, that's it. And unfortunately, because Darius is my client, it just doesn't work. We'll have to revisit the idea of me and him being together when SCI finishes his project."

"Here comes my unsolicited advice, but first I'll start by saying I understand your logic and that women do have a tougher time in this industry, but you can't help who you fall in love with."

"No one said anything about—"

"As long as you're not frolicking around on the job, keep your personal life personal. Know how and when to draw the line."

"And that's exactly what I did." Kennedy interrupted again. "His project was getting behind schedule, and—"

"From something that was beyond your control. Kennedy, you're smart enough not to let your relationship get in the way of work. Is there something else you're not telling me?"

It felt silly to actually speak aloud that she had strong feelings for a man she'd only known a few months and that merely being in the same room with him made her insides melt. To tell anyone that his eyes found their way into her dreams every night since the moment they'd met would probably earn her a ticket to the house for the mentally unstable. The way her name rolled off his lips sent a shiver through her ears and pierced her heart. And don't even get her started on the fireworks that were set off whenever he touched her hand or wrapped his arms around her in one of those bear hugs. Nope, there was nothing else she cared to share.

"That's it. You know we can't mess this project up. Our reputation would be ruined if anything goes wrong that we can't handle. But on the flipside, just think of how business would skyrocket when we knock this thing out the park. Kendrick would be so happy about this."

Mabel nodded. "Yes, he would, except he isn't here. Kennedy, it's time you start making business and personal decisions based on what you desire, not according to what

Kendrick would want. I know he'd love for you to put your sparkle on this place. His memory will forever live on through you, but you don't have to make choices the way you think he would in order to do that."

By this time, she got that stinging feeling in her nostrils, and tears threatened to stream down her cheeks. Mabel took hold of her hands again and squeezed.

"Do me this one favor: Pray about how you should proceed with SCI and how you need to handle your relationship with Darius. In Psalm 138:8, the Bible tells us that God will perfect that which concerns us, meaning He will work out His plans for your life, but you need to submit to Him. I just love you, and I want to see you live your life to the fullest, as you young people like to say."

One sniff, and tears trickled down her cheeks. "I just can't mess this up. For me or for Darius. If we can just make it through this, then everything will work itself out."

Mabel snatched two sheets of tissues from the box on Kennedy's desk and beelined to Kennedy's side, dabbing her wet cheeks. "You're stronger than you think, smarter than you give yourself credit for, and successful in your own right. I just want you happy and soaring in your purpose—your purpose, not Kendrick's."

Mabel comforted her in silence with her arms snug around Kennedy's shoulders. Mabel's truth serum seeped down into her heart, but she couldn't quite deviate from the path she believed would give her success with this project and ultimately with Darius. Kennedy's sniffles settled, and she gave Mabel's arm a final pat to release her.

"Thank you, Auntie. I'll pray about it."

Mabel kissed the top of her head and stood. "You do that. God won't steer you wrong, but whatever way He leads, I hope you listen. I don't think I can take much more of you moping around here."

Kennedy pouted and pursed her lips. "Hey, I'm not that bad, and besides, I haven't been moping, just focused."

Mabel squeezed her shoulders and sauntered to the door. "Just focus on getting your life together is all I'm saying. Be back in forty-five minutes," Mabel tossed over her shoulder before she exited and shut the door behind her.

Kennedy unearthed her cell phone from the desk drawer, pressed it beneath her chin, and debated whether she should call Darius or Nina. She whispered a prayer and afterward unlocked her screen to call Darius, but was interrupted by the ringing of her desk phone.

"This is Kennedy. How may I help you?"

"Miss Slaughter, I am Fitz Crudup, CEO of Stallion Fitness. I wanted to reach out to you myself and request that your team throw your hat in the ring for an expansion project we're planning in Houston, Dallas, and Austin. A friend of a friend is impressed with the work SCI is doing on the McCall project, and I'd like the opportunity to work with you, if possible."

"Thank you for reaching out to me, Mr. Crudup." Kennedy quickly keyed his name and business into the Google search engine, and her heart stopped for several seconds, she was sure of it. Fitz Crudup was the wealthiest fitness center operator in America. Securing a job like that one would give SCI exposure beyond her imagination— she'd have to expand the business. Kennedy took a deep breath to reel her thoughts back into the present. The first step was to bid on the job and secure it.

"Thank you for considering the opportunity."

Kennedy and Fitz talked a few minutes longer about key details regarding the project before he ended the call with promises to have his assistant e-mail her additional details. Kennedy's hands trembled, and she fumbled with the phone before successfully hanging it up. The e-mail came through immediately, and she scanned it before sending it to Chris and Mike with a proposed meeting time to discuss.

She leaped out of her seat and twirled around her office, correlating the good news with the fact that she put work first, trusted her instincts, and kept her mind focused on the McCall project. Though a sense of relief and accomplishment settled within her, it didn't feel quite like she thought it would.

Elated yet not quite satisfied.

Perhaps Mabel was right, and she'd been a little too focused on work, not making time for the things or the person who mattered.

Kennedy grabbed her phone again to call Darius. He was the first person she wanted to share the good news with, but she put the phone down. She had to do what she promised Mabel: pray first.

# Twenty

After the birth of his nephew and Andrew's decision to transition out of his role as CEO, Darius remained in Georgia until the completion of the Houston project. That way Kennedy could focus on her work with little interference from him, he could transition into his new role as CEO, and everyone could get what they wanted. Their weekly meetings were reduced to phone calls or Zoom when necessary. He'd traveled back to Houston three times in the last three months—once to get his things and the other two times for a site visit.

Every time he saw Kennedy, his heart broke in two. One thing that had proven to be a lie was that with time he'd get over her and just move on. As much as his heart needed that to be true, it couldn't have been farther from it. Crazy how she had that effect on him, and he didn't like it one bit. *Be patient. Give her time.* None of which had seemed to work up to this point.

Today would make the fourth time he'd seen her in person since he'd returned home.

Thankfully, the construction delays they'd experienced weren't detrimental to their target December completion.

McCall Resorts Houston's grand opening was at the end of the week, and Darius' flight to Houston departed in less than an hour. He attempted to fixate his attention on all things McCall Resorts to keep his mind off Kennedy and how she'd respond to seeing him again and whether it would be wise for them to pick up where they left off or simply let it all go.

At boarding call, he went through the necessary steps to board the plane until he found himself seated in first class. His heart nearly leaped in his throat when the woman who claimed the seat in front of him reminded him of Kennedy—same height, hair texture, skin color, and even her perfume was close enough to the scent he'd dubbed as her signature fragrance.

He removed his phone from his suit jacket to do something he hadn't done in a while—call Kennedy for a reason other than a business discussion.

"Hey, I'm on a plane headed to Houston to prepare for the grand opening at the end of the week. Are you available for dinner tonight?"

"I would love to, really, but I'm kind of stuck at home today. My yardman has been a no-show for the past four weeks, and I've already received two letters from the homeowner's association. I'm in the middle of trying to find someone to get over here today, and I'm having plumbing issues, too. Waiting on the plumber to come over now. I promise I'm not making excuses, but I just have a lot going on. Raincheck?"

"Raincheck. Is there anything I can do to help?"

"Unless you know a plumber or a lawn guy, I don't think so."

"I'll take care of the lawn situation for you when I get there. Depending on the plumbing issue, I can handle that, too." It had to have been nearly twenty years since he'd touched a lawnmower, but for Kennedy, he'd do anything. Plumbing skills, he picked up when their resort was limited to a bed-and-breakfast with only one estate house. If it was something minor, he could do the work.

"But how are—"

"Time to power down my phone. I'll call you when I land."

"Alrighty then. Have a safe flight."

Darius ended the call and placed a pickup order for a lawnmower, tools, and a toolbox from the nearest home improvement retailer. Satisfied with himself, he set his phone to airplane mode, tucked it away, and nestled himself comfortably in his oversized leather seat. If he planned to push a lawnmower in a few hours, he may as well pre-rest. Unsure of how to tag his feelings for her, he realized they had to go beyond *like* if he was willing to voluntarily do manual labor.

∞

The cranking of a lawnmower snatched Kennedy's attention away from her laptop. She trudged to peep out the window, thinking her lawn guy had finally gotten her hundreds of messages. She didn't know what to think about that. It wasn't like she didn't pay him timely. Not only did she pay him, but she also left a hefty tip along with bottles of water inside a cooler next to her front door for him on lawn days.

When she separated the blinds, it wasn't George she saw. Dressed in a pair of jeans that were too nice for yardwork, Darius pushed the lawnmower back and forth through her yard, and her heart softened. He hadn't even called to tell her he'd landed in Houston like he'd promised.

With one disaster to deal with after another, she'd lost track of time.

Kennedy took one look at her own bleach-stained yoga pants and oversized t-shirt and scurried to the bathroom to freshen up and change her attire. She shuffled to the kitchen to grab a bottled water out of the refrigerator. Seventy degrees during the month of December made for pleasant weather, but the least she could do was show she appreciated Darius for going out of his way to help her.

A heap of guilt cluttered her mind as she paused at the front door, hand resting on the knob. Three months ago, Mabel encouraged her to pray about her relationship with Darius and about the direction she needed to take SCI. She'd done so on many occasions, but as time went on, she couldn't bring herself to pick up the phone to talk to him about anything more than business.

Maybe fear stood in her way.

Fear of where it would lead.

She couldn't be sure she was ready. Would she have to push the pause button on their relationship again, frustrating them both even more?

But something stirred within her at the sight of him trekking back and forth in her yard, an activity she would have pegged him as thinking was beneath him. Surely, he could find someone to pay to handle such a task, but he did it himself. She had to give him his props. Whenever she opened herself up to the opportunity, he consistently proved he cared about her. She closed her eyes and whispered a quick prayer, hoping that it wasn't too late for her to show him she cared about him, too.

Kennedy whipped opened the door and scurried up alongside him with the bottled water.

"Thought you could use this."

He accepted it and took a long swig. The smile that illuminated his face afterward ignited the arteries that pumped blood through her veins.

"Thank you."

Kennedy brushed the water droplets from his thin mustache. "I should be thanking you."

He raised a suggestive eyebrow and charmed her with a full set of pearly whites. "Dinner?"

"I'll take care of it."

"Appreciate that. I'm losing daylight, so let me finish out here, then I'll check on your plumbing issue."

Kennedy's eyes roamed his face and settled on his lips. Now was the perfect moment to finally see how his lips felt against hers, but she controlled herself. For one, she was outside and wasn't the type of person to give her neighbors a show. And two, they hadn't established where they would go from here after not dating the past few months.

"You're the best. Just come inside when you're done."

Kennedy sauntered back into the house on jelly-like legs, praying he wasn't watching her walk away. Inside the house, she crashed on the living room sofa and buried her head in a throw pillow. Why did it feel like she was losing her mind? This should not be difficult. He had been what was missing from her life the past few months, and she suddenly felt like a fool for stepping away. But if she hadn't, would she have been able to focus on work and perform the way she had?

And now that prospective clients with larger jobs were seeking them out, just as she'd hoped, there was still an emptiness inside her that couldn't be replaced with larger contracts, exercise, or any other activity. Deep in her soul, she knew what she craved, but she couldn't quite bring herself to acknowledge that it was him. She was an educated, successful woman. Yet, her aunt Mabel's words rang in her hear: *There's more to life than work.* She didn't need a man to be happy, but her very being craved Darius like a woman craves chocolate during that time of the month.

*This is crazy.*

But decisions needed to be made about where they would go from here, even though he would be leaving for Atlanta permanently after the grand opening of the resort on Friday.

In five days.

A strong voice within her screamed to leave things as they were to protect herself from the inevitable heartache that was sure to follow when they could no longer make their relationship work due to the long distance.

*I'm not gonna assume. I'll make the choice with him this time.*

That settled it.

Kennedy rummaged through her pantry and freezer to see if she had anything that she could whip up within the next hour or so to double as gratitude for Darius volunteering his services today and to show off her culinary skills. Frozen poultry and beef would take too long to thaw, and she wasn't in the mood for fish, which probably wouldn't be too filling for Darius after yardwork. Kennedy then sifted through her junk drawer for one of those advertising door hangers for Chinese food. The thought of fried rice and egg rolls made her stomach turn cartwheels. She placed an order for delivery, and Darius tapped on the front door three times before entering as she ended her call.

Sweaty with grass-stained jeans and a toolbox in his hand, Darius closed the door behind him and removed his shoes. "Point me to your plumbing problem."

If it were physically possible, Kennedy's heart would've melted, turned solid, and then melted again at the sight of him. Never mind the fact he wasn't dressed like someone prepared to do yard or plumbing work, he went the extra step to purchase the lawnmower and tools to ensure he got the jobs done.

"Right this way." Kennedy led him to her powder room where she explained the clogged toilet and sink needed service. He nodded his understanding. She stepped to the side and watched while he went to work. First, he shut off the water valve and then removed the pipes under the sink.

Kennedy didn't know much about plumbing work, but prayed he did because she couldn't take it if he created a bigger mess. Though secretly, she was overly impressed by his willingness to help her.

"I'm curious as to how you know anything about plumbing."

Without turning to look at her, he kept his attention focused on the task ahead of him. "Yeah, I learned early on while working alongside my dad. I was about twelve, I think, and we were only a bed-and-breakfast, which consisted of one estate house with seven rooms. I watched him fix toilets many days until I learned myself. It isn't difficult." He pointed to the PVC pipe and explained why he pulled it apart, the cleaning that needed to take place, and how to do it.

"I don't think I'll be cleaning pipes. I think I'll just call you next time."

"That's all you have to do is call, and I'll be here." This time he stopped and offered a lingering gaze, which sent a movement down her spine, much like a trickle of water. Kennedy shivered and backed into the hallway.

"That's good to know. Let me get out of your way. I'll just be in the kitchen waiting for you when you're done."

Thirty minutes later, Darius emerged from the bathroom and announced, "Your powder room is back in business. Mind if I use one of your showers to clean myself up?"

"Of course not, especially after the favors you've done for me today." Kennedy waved her hand. "You can use or have whatever you want around here right about now."

Darius smirked, and she knew her word choice had gotten her into trouble. "I'll hold you to that. Let me run to the car and grab my things. Be right back."

He returned within the minute with brown paper bags. "Is this what I think it is?"

"Yes. Fried rice for me and chow mein with beef and chicken for you."

"What are you trying to do to me, woman? You know I love Chinese food, and I haven't had my fix since the last time we went out."

Kennedy's smile faded, and she waited for a reaction from him.

"I didn't mean it like that. Lighten up."

"I know. I'll take these. Go ahead and get cleaned up so we can eat...and talk."

Darius handed her the food and leaned in and kissed her forehead before disappearing outside again. Forehead kisses, as she'd known them, were meant to be friendly, unpassionate, but that kiss was everything but that. She stood in the same space, unable to move, the imprint of his lips melting her skin and sending warning signals to her heart. He missed her as much as she missed him, maybe more.

"You okay?"

She'd been so zoned out that she didn't see or hear him come back inside, and he was in her line of vision. His voice broke the spell his forehead kiss put her under, and she jerked and turned away from him to place the food on the island. She kept her back to him for fear he would identify every emotion she felt by looking into her eyes. "Just thinking about what movie we could watch." She pointed. "Shower is the second door to your right."

"Thanks. Be back shortly."

When she heard the door close, she gripped the corners of the island, slumped her shoulders, and took a few deep, focused breaths. *Just have the conversation with him and get it over with.*

Holding her feelings inside had done nothing but drive her mad. If she kept it up, the man was probably going to think she was out of her mind. Shoot, if she didn't know herself, she would think that about herself since she'd been acting weird since he'd shown up. He obviously cared a great deal for her, and he'd been demonstrating it for the last three hours.

Kennedy busied herself setting the table with plates, glasses, napkins, and silverware. She could no longer hear the shower stream and took the opportunity to mentally rehearse her speech. No matter if they talked and decided that being together wouldn't work for them—that it was too late—she couldn't let the night end without trying her best to express what he meant to her.

"I'm ready for that talk now."

Kennedy turned around to face him, braced herself against the chair, and froze, though her heart didn't get the message. His lips parted into a crooked smile like he knew the conversation was about to go his way, but one look at him, and all the words she planned to say escaped her.

# Twenty-one

That was probably the quickest shower Darius had taken in his entire life.

Pushing a mower up and down Kennedy's lawn gave him more than enough time to muddle over their situation. They were meant to be together. The only thing left to do was get Kennedy in agreement. Ordinarily, he wouldn't have given a woman a second thought if she wanted to pause their relationship, but with Kennedy, he hadn't been able to think about anyone but her. He'd even gone out with another woman, but it wasn't enough because she wasn't Kennedy.

Kennedy busied herself removing takeout boxes from the delivery bags, avoiding eye contact with him as much as possible. Darius reached out, took her jittery hands in his, and led her to the living room sofa. He sat on the coffee table in front of her and lifted her chin with his fingertip.

"Kennedy, I don't know any other way to have this conversation, but to be honest with you." His heart thumped dramatically in his ears, like drums, yet he continued in hopes of silencing the near-deafening sound. "I've had a lot of time to think about you—well, about us—over the past few months. I wanted to forget about you and the connection I thought we shared, but I haven't been able to shake it. I've tried dating another woman thinking that maybe I'd become lonely, and I only needed company, but that wasn't it."

The light in her eyes dimmed when he mentioned another woman, and his heart cinched. He rubbed his chest to ease the physical manifestation of the pain.

"Kennedy, only you can quench the thirst in my heart."

Kennedy's eyes lit up again, and she chuckled.

"I'm serious. That line may be a little corny, but it's fitting. I've missed you, and I want us to find a way to work this out and be together. Project or no project. Client or not."

"I've missed you, too, Darius." She took hold of his hands and squeezed. "The truth is, many times over the last few months, I've wanted to come to you, to tell you I'd changed my mind, but then SCI received a request to bid on a large project, so I thought it had to be because I was concentrating more on work."

"Kennedy, you know you're amazing, right, and I don't want to do anything that will stand in the way of you accomplishing your goals. If anything, I hope that my being in your life will encourage you and help push you to achieve whatever it is that you want to go for. I'd never be a hindrance to you. I believe the success of SCI would've happened, even if we were together."

Kennedy nodded. "I believe that now. I'm just sorry it took me so long to realize it."

Darius searched her eyes—the depths of them called to him. "So can we be together?"

"I want to be with you, but how do we make a long-distance relationship work? Aren't you headed back to Georgia after the grand opening?"

"Yes, but I don't want to use distance as an excuse. I can fly out here to visit every weekend if necessary."

"But is that realistic? You'll get tired of that, and then where will that leave us?"

"We'll find a way. Trust me. That's one thing I know to be true. We all make time and adjustments in our lives for what we want. We don't have to figure it all out right now—all I want to hear is that you want to be with me like I need to be with you. We can deal with the rest as it comes."

"I want to be with you. I just hate that I allowed all this time to pass and—"

Darius crushed his lips against hers, savoring the taste of her strawberry-flavored lip gloss. Kennedy cupped his jaw, and he just about lost it. The electricity that sizzled between them cut through every inch of him, from his head to his fingertips, down to the soles of his feet. His heart swelled so, he thought it might burst. The friction in his chest was unbearable, so he broke the kiss. Kennedy licked her lips, and he thought it might be the end of him.

"Then, it's settled. You and me."

To keep from making a move they might regret later, he stood and intertwined his hand with hers, leading her back to the kitchen for dinner.

The spark he'd become accustomed to seeing in her eyes returned, which made him glad he chose to try one last time with her before giving up for good and burying his feelings. Their evening evolved into one well spent with them talking, laughing, and enjoying each other as if no time had passed. After dinner, with Kennedy's feet propped on his lap, they settled down on the sofa for a movie. Kennedy roped him into watching one of those Hallmark movies, and he couldn't help but think about his mom and dad—now his father enjoyed those predictable happily-ever-after movies. He wouldn't become that guy, but he could now understand how a man would do anything for the woman he loved.

Darius nearly choked on air at the thought, slapping his chest a couple of times. Falling in love just wasn't something he did, but if this was what it felt like… His heart was now content, and his mind was at peace. He'd give it a go with Kennedy.

∞

The day had finally come.

The remainder of the McCall family joined Darius in Houston for the resort's grand opening. Darius circled around the fishbowl of a conference room decorated with Christmas garland, a replica of the Atlanta conference room, his chest puffed and a job-well-done smile plastered across his face.

He was about to officially be named CEO, but it didn't feel as good as he thought it would. That power he'd craved for so long wasn't enough, especially if it meant returning to Atlanta and living his life as he'd done before he met Kennedy.

He'd reconciled with the woman who'd stolen his heart. It was time he rearranged his priorities. He still desired to lead McCall Resorts, but giving his relationship with Kennedy a chance to thrive was equally important. How could he have both?

"Son," Jeffrey strode in, his voice leading the way, with Rose, Andrew, Nina, and Andrew Jr. following, "I'm proud of you. You visualized it and saw it through to the end." Jeffrey rhythmically slapped him on the back.

Rose moved to the opposite side of him and wrapped her arms around his waist. "Yes, it's just like home, except what we'll be producing on the farm. I'm proud of you, son."

Nina piped in, "Is Kennedy stopping by today?"

All eyes were on him. The mere mention of her name made his heart write its own song.

Darius flipped his wrist to check the time. "Yeah. She should be here any minute now."

"So, you two made up or what?"

Andrew nudged Nina's arm and shot her a warning look. Clearly, his love life was at the forefront of all their minds with the way their eyes were glued on him, waiting for any news about his relationship with Kennedy. "Yes, we did. We're gonna work it out."

Rose pumped a fist in the air. "Yes. I called it. I knew she was the one."

Darius frowned. "What do you mean?"

Jeffrey jumped in. "What she means is that the whole reason we went with SCI is because your mother saw a picture of the president—Kennedy—did a little Google search on her and found out she was single, so in hopes that you two would hit it off, we accepted their bid for the job, and the rest is history. Too much Hallmark. Told you."

"But hey, it worked out." Rose gestured toward Darius like a game show model. "Look at his face. Those wrinkles in his forehead we're so used to seeing have disappeared. He's happy, he's lighter. This was good for him."

The McCall family erupted into laughter. Darius wanted to be upset, but how could he? He never would have found Kennedy if it weren't for his mother's meddling. He could forgive her this one time.

"I guess I'll give you a pass, Mom. Drew, did you know about this?"

Andrew shook his head. "Not until you brought her home."

Jeffrey held his palms up, drawing everyone's attention. "The ribbon cutting is in an hour, but since we're all here, let's sit and discuss business for a few minutes."

When the family gathered around the table, Jeffrey continued, and directed his attention toward Darius. "Son, when this project started, I made a deal with you that if you could see this through to completion, grow from the experience, and learn to play well with others, then I'd consider naming you as my successor—if Andrew decided he wanted something different."

Darius interrupted. "Hold on, Dad. Can I say something?"

Jeffrey nodded.

"I've given this a lot of thought over the past month or so, and I like the idea of the joint CEO strategy with Drew, if he can agree to that. I can run the Houston resort while Drew handles business back in Atlanta. Like a Netflix sort of structure."

The sharp intake of air from everyone in the room caused a bubble of laughter to erupt from his belly. "Dang, y'all acting like I just told y'all I killed somebody."

"What happened to you out here, bro?"

"Man, it's just that I realized that other things are important, too, and I think we can take this company far if we work together."

Kennedy happened.

Because of her, he wanted more than to be CEO. He worked alongside his father long enough to know that being the CEO often came with sacrifices, and if he could split the duties with his brother, Andrew could have time with his growing family, and he could give his relationship with Kennedy the time it deserved.  He chuckled again, but this time at himself. How had that woman changed him?

"So, Dad, Drew, will that work for the two of you?"

Jeffrey nodded toward Andrew, who looked to Nina and obviously found encouragement from her nod and smile. Andrew Jr. squealed. "The Mrs. and the little guy are in agreement, so I don't think I can say no to that. You've got yourself a joint CEO if that's okay with Dad."

"That was actually going to be my suggestion. I know that Andrew considered stepping down because he wanted to be there for Andrew Jr. and Nina, so this way it works out for everyone involved, including me. I can now transition into retirement a happy man, knowing my sons will work together for the good of the business."

Rose reached across the table and squeezed Darius' hands. "I am one proud momma. To say I've been worried about you and this path you've been on is putting it lightly, but you surprised me, and that makes my heart happy. I'll miss you back home, but this move is good for you." She squeezed one last time, winked, and pulled away.

He rubbed the knot positioned at the base of his throat and cleared it. "Thanks, Mom. You know I'll be back to visit often, but I think this is the best way to give everyone what they want and need."

On cue, Kennedy appeared outside the conference room and waved.

"I think that's our signal to leave." Rose stood. "Thirty-five minutes until ribbon cutting. Don't take too long."

Jeffrey stood, rounded the table, and held out his arm for Rose, and they left the room. Darius halted Andrew and Nina's departure. He sucked the air between his teeth and drew in a deep breath. He placed a hand on each of their shoulders. "Drew and Nina, I owe both of you an apology. Nina, I see now that you love my brother, and you've got his back. You can't blame me for doubting you, but I'm glad he has you."

Nina put Andrew Jr. in his father's arms and hugged Darius' neck. "I know I messed up before, but I do love him, and I love you, too, brother-in-law. Hopefully, we can work our way back to being friends again. We'll miss your antics in Atlanta, but I know that Kennedy will hold you down here." Then she whispered, "Don't mess this up. I want a sister-in-law."

He broke their embrace. "Drew, ban her from watching Hallmark movies or reading those romance novels."

Andrew laughed, and Nina tagged his shoulder. "Whatever. Just remember what I said. See you downstairs."

"And Drew, I know I've been acting crazy about this whole thing, so please accept my apology. I'm trying to be a better man."

Andrew glanced toward Kennedy who stood just outside the door with her head down texting. "I bet you are. Just remember, it's not a competition between us. We're brothers, man. And I'm staying because I want to do my part in mending this family—never to undermine you. One day, I'll teach again, but for now, you're stuck with me."

"I get it, bro." Darius took Andrew's hand in a firm grip. "Oh, it's always a competition."

Andrew chuckled and shook his head. "*Tsk. Tsk.* See you downstairs."

A weight had been lifted off Darius' shoulders.

Kennedy entered when Andrew and Nina cleared the room. Darius perched on the edge of the conference room table and extended his hands to hers. When they connected, warmth sizzled up his arm, and he broke into an I've-got-something-special-to-share-with-you-and-I-know-you're-gonna-love-it smile.

"It's nice to see you, too. Ready for the ribbon cutting ceremony? I figured we could go together."

"You figured right, but first I have something to tell you." Darius bit down on his bottom lip and gazed into her eyes—eyes he could swim in if possible.

"Don't tease me. What's up?"

"Christmas came about two weeks early this year. My father just named me CEO."

Kennedy threw her arms around his neck, stomping her feet. "Congrats. I'm so proud of you." She pulled away, but her arms remained locked around his neck. "We knew that would happen because you're so amazing. How do you want to celebrate?"

Kennedy was close enough for him to kiss her, though he held back when all he wanted to do in that moment was feel her lips against his. "That's not all. I'm actually joint CEO with Drew. He and I both agreed to it. The terms will have to be ironed out later, but I'm confident we can make it work."

"So, you worked things out with your brother. That's even better—worth more than you becoming CEO."

"I can agree with that. If I haven't learned anything else throughout this process, I've learned that relationships are important, so here's the best part."

Kennedy squeezed his neck. "You mean there's more? What else could you possibly need?"

He tilted his head toward her and gave her one of those you-are-what-else-I-could-possibly-need looks. "I'll be doing my part right here in Houston, so all those questions you had about whether or not our relationship could survive long distance are no longer relevant. I'll be in Houston permanently."

Kennedy blinked back tears and fanned her eyes. "Darius, you didn't do this for me, did you?"

"Nope."

Her eyes bucked, and he doubled over in laughter. "I did it for us. I love you, Kennedy Slaughter, and I want to do everything within my power to give us a fair shot."

"I love you, too, Darius. I don't think I could've asked for a better Christmas present."

"Me either."

Darius gave in to his desire and pulled Kennedy closer into a long-awaited kiss. That same sizzling spark that ignited within him the moment their hands touched the first time was alive and blazing. He broke the kiss and rested his forehead against hers—every organ within his chest near explosion, a feeling he never wanted to come down from. Without a doubt, this would be the best Christmas he'd ever had given he received everything he wanted and everything he didn't know he needed.

Dear reader,

I hope you enjoyed Darius and Kennedy's story as much as I enjoyed writing it. I have to say that this is my favorite series to date. As of now, there is one more book in the works for this series. So do stick around to see what happens between Kennedy's cousin, Mike and Nina's assistant, Danielle.

P.S. Please consider leaving a review on Goodreads/Bookbub/Amazon.

Thank you for your support!

*Natasha*

**About the Author**

Natasha writes Christian fiction and devotionals. When she isn't reading or writing, she spends her time working out, swimming or watching movies with her family. She lives in the Houston metro area with her husband and three children.

Connect with Natasha online:

Bookbub @NatashaDFrazier
Instagram @author_natashafrazier
Twitter @author_natashaf
Facebook @craves.2012
Website: www.natashafrazier.com

Natasha D. Frazier

# Other titles by Natasha D. Frazier

## _Devotionals_

_The Life Your Spirit Craves_

_Not Without You_

_Not Without You Prayer Journal_

_The Life Your Spirit Craves for Mommies_

_Pursuit_

## _Fiction_

_Love, Lies & Consequences_

_Through Thick & Thin: Love, Lies & Consequences Book 2_

_Shattered Vows: Love, Lies & Consequences Book 3_

_Out of the Shadows: Love, Lies & Consequences Book 4_

_Kairos: The Perfect Time for Love_

_Fate (The Perfect Time for Love series)_

_With Every Breath (McCall Family Series Book 1)_

## _Non-Fiction_

_How Long Are You Going to Wait?_

www.ingramcontent.com/pod-product-compliance
Lightning Source LLC
Chambersburg PA
CBHW022014120726
47902CB00012B/170